I0619231

GLOW GRASS

and other tales

M.H. CALLWAY

Glow Grass and Other Tales

M.H. Callway

Print Edition 2016

ISBN 13: 978-1-77242-047-0

Carrick Publishing

Copyright M.H. Callway 2016

Cover Photo by Edward G. Callway

Cover design by Sara Carrick

This book is intended for your personal enjoyment only. This book may not be sold or given away to other people. If you did not purchase this book, or it was not purchased for your use only, then please return to Amazon.com and purchase your own copy. Thank you for respecting the hard work of this author.

The characters and situations described within this book are fictional. They are creations of the author's imagination and do not represent real persons or events in any way.

CONTENTS

With love to Claire and Mitch

FOREWORD

Greetings Readers!

This book contains nine of my published stories to entertain and beguile you, from comedy to dark suspense.

Because I write noir, most of my stories have a darker bent. Most deal with overcoming a serious threat – threats like career death in "The Dog on Balmy Beach" to cold-hearted murder in the novella, "Glow Grass". How the central character confronts their dire fate forms the basis of each story. Will they beat the odds against them or succumb? Will they be killed or be driven to murder? Dive into these pages to find out!

Two comic tales, "Kill the Boss" and "Amdur's Cat", bookend the collection. Both stories were inspired by my work experience in government bureaucracy. *Yes, Minister* is not a joke – it's my belief that the writers simply recorded actual happenings. I leave it to you, dear readers, to decide if the events I portray are true or merely revenge fantasies conjured up by a beleaguered minion's brain.

For those interested, many of the stories won or were short-listed for awards, including: the Arthur Ellis, the Derringer and the Bony Pete.

I would love to hear from you. Visit my website at www.mhcallway.com where I blog regularly about crime fiction (Eat This Book), Toronto street art (Wanderings), strange urban encounters (Surreal Trapdoor) and the fascinating people in my life (Cyber Café). You may also follow me on Facebook and Twitter (@mcallway).

Enjoy the ride!

M. H. Callway

M.H. CALLWAY

KILL THE BOSS

My experience in government bureaucracy inspired this story, together with a newspaper article about a woman who deceived her colleagues for years.

Published in Silver Moon Magazine, *January, 2006 and reprinted in* Mouth Full of Bullets, *September, 2007.*

Winner of the Golden Horseshoe Award, 2005, a short story contest sponsored by the Crime Writers of Canada, Ontario Region.

"I hate my job," I said. "Truly, madly, deeply. With passion and conviction."

Bertie, my cell-mate in our office's maze of cloth-covered boxes, sighed, smoothed back her spiky red hair, and granted me her usual look of benign indulgence. "Lorraine, consider the alternative. Unemployment. You're just upset about turning 50. You'll get over it."

Would I? No one hires people over 50, especially as civil servants. And men don't date women over 40. Since my divorce, even the possibility of charity sex looked bleak. My ears were ringing with the sound of the doors of opportunity slamming shut.

"Think about the French pastry shop we'll be raiding for your birthday lunch," Bertie said. "Think white wine, raspberries and crème fraîche. It'll get us through the staff meeting Magda called this morning."

More good news. "Was she really in at 7 am?"

"Yep." Bertie hammered away at her keyboard in her longstanding battle with our dysfunctional computer network. "On her way in, she just happened to mention that she has a day nanny *and* a night nanny."

For reasons known only to our fusty Assistant Deputy Minister, Dr. Vladimir Nickle, our Policy Coordination Unit served as the gateway to the great Snakes and Ladders game of senior management. All aspiring careerists passed through us on their way up to – or hurtling down from – the corporate stratosphere. Magda was our newly appointed director.

To save our sanity, over the years Bertie and I had devised a boss-cataloguing system. Fiery prodigies who spring-boarded through in sojourns of mere weeks, we named The Comets. Those who fell from grace, we called The Meteors. And Magda's predecessor, who'd hidden under his desk before vanishing on permanent stress leave, we'd baptized The Black Hole. But classifying the enigmatic Magda Molina had proved difficult, so temporarily we'd labelled her the Quasar.

But I'm not a naïve fool. By 50, I should hope not! I'd already ferreted out my moles in the division to glean vital info on her management style. After all, forewarned is forearmed. But curiously, so far I'd got nothing. Even Ramona, our admin assistant, landed Magda's official backgrounder before I did. Together with everyone else, I learned that the Quasar was a graduate of Toronto's high-ranking Mendelssohn Business School and that she shared a Rosedale mansion with her young family.

Analysis: she didn't need to work for a living. She was in the job for love.

This was not a plus.

Just the same, I tried to like and respect Magda. Really I did. Her warm smile charmed me, especially when she spoke about her children. One daughter was a prodigy at the

National Ballet School, the other a bourgeoning artist though still in Montessori kindergarten. And she often mentioned the charities she and her corporate executive husband supported – as well as the vivid succession of balls, concerts, and celebrity golf tournaments they had to attend. Surely her devotion to social causes made her human…

"Have a chocolate, doctor's orders," Bertie said, prying open the box of truffles Ramona had brought in for my birthday. "I struck gold today."

Covering my eagerness to hear the tidbit of gossip she'd landed, I snagged a truffle that bristled with chocolate shavings like a hedgehog.

Bertie's grin grew foxier. "Magda is Vlad the Spellchecker's prodigy."

Disaster! I stuffed down three more of those babies.

Dr. Nickle – Vlad the Spellchecker to us – had ruled our division for 25 years, his astonishing longevity cemented by his mastery of the art of obstructionism. Stifling innovation meant no programs, and no programs meant no problems for our political masters. They all loved him. The few contentious issues that did squeak through from the public sank in Vlad's miry sea of government-speak. Starting at 7 each morning, he edited every report, letter and memo that emanated from our division. In detail. He'd reject correspondence for a comma which – inevitably — mutated into a moving target. My personal record for the number of back and forth journeys of a draft letter between our office and his stood at 16.

Damn! I grabbed another three mother's little helpers from the chocolate box.

Vlad's disciple. Oh God, that meant Magda was *connected*. We'd be powerless no matter how bizarre she turned out to be. And if she decided to downsize us, we didn't have a prayer.

Queasy now, I trailed into the boardroom for our staff meeting and slumped down next to Bertie. Magda's wonderful smile sought me out. I smiled back. Why was her well-manicured finger tracing an ellipse next to her mouth? Mimicking her unconsciously, I dislodged a chocolate shaving clinging to my cheek. I felt uncomfortably hot, and not just from middle age.

When we'd all settled into our chairs, Magda smiled sweetly at our admin assistant and said, "Ramona, this meeting is only for professional staff. I thought you would have understood that."

Face red, Ramona pushed back her chair and left. The rest of us stared down at our notepads and pens. Disgracefully, we said nothing.

"I'm so sorry to make this a short meeting," Magda went on, "but I'm seeing my daughters' allergist this morning." She paused to smooth back an invisible strand of shiny chestnut hair. "They're highly attuned to chemical toxins in the environment. Everything they touch has to be pure, completely organic."

I could have sworn Bertie muttered something like 'my ass'.

Magda stretched back, looking at each of us in turn. "So do forgive me if I appear to be brutally frank, but truth is best. Dr. Nickle is deeply concerned about your unit."

Those nicely digesting truffles congealed into a tarry mass.

"You all risk embarrassing the Minister with your undisciplined writing."

Hot acrid chocolate burned the back of my throat. Embarrass the Minister? Collectively, we had a century of government experience! I braced myself for that dreaded word: reorganization.

"Clearly, you all have forgotten how to write."

Oh, no, much worse! Under her elegant hand, I spotted an ominously familiar, mustard-hued booklet: the *Ministry Guide to Style*, penned by Vlad the Spellchecker himself.

"I have no choice but to sign off on all your correspondence personally. And I only look at hard copy."

"But our office is fully electronic," Roger, our Senior IT Manager, protested.

"I'm aware of that, but hard copy unlocks the mind's creative potential," Magda countered. "Each letter you write must be flawless: warm, caring and personal. Mine your creativity. Some of you will have to dig rather deeply, but do look upon it as a challenge."

I coughed. Bertie kicked me under the table. Hard.

Again that warm smile. "I shall be coaching each of you. Personally."

I threw up. Oh, not there in Magda's boardroom, though arguably charging out of the meeting to plunge into the washroom counted as a heinous career-limiting move. Later, Bertie tracked me down in the stalls to deliver the *coup de grace*. After I'd bolted from the room, Magda had limited our lunch breaks to the exact 45 minutes set out by the Ministry's guidelines.

And so my exquisitely anticipated birthday lunch became our unit's first casualty.

"Magda's not a Quasar," I fumed over a limp salad in the food court after work. "She's a Supernova, a cosmic disaster. I can't afford to lose my job. My divorce lawyer bankrupted me."

"I should never have moved to the Beaches," Bertie sighed. "Dream house, mean mortgage. If I quit, I lose everything."

"She'll drive us mad. Oh, heavens, we can't just sit here and complain. We have to *do* something."

Bertie rubbed her crimson spikes, thinking. "OK, here's the deal. We wait until she leaves the office. We go down to the parking lot, leap into my car and then…we *kill* her."

"Be serious!"

"Who's joking?" Bertie looked foxier than ever. "Let's make it our Special Project. We'll call it long-term strategic planning."

Sometimes Bertie really is too much, I thought later as I trudged to the subway through the dust thrown up by the demolition next to our office. The much unlamented red-brick Government Archives building was being knocked down to make way for a sleek condo tower. Today its destruction seemed a sinister prophecy. Had I, too, become disposable, languishing away at the Ministry, sacrificing my dreams for financial security?

Happy 50th birthday, I thought, fighting through the rush hour crowd on the subway stairs. Heading back to a dingy apartment I could barely afford. No spare cash for hobbies or vacations. My job devolving into a torture chamber. But as I clung to the sticky overhand rail bracing myself against the train's sway, my passionate words to Bertie came back to haunt me. Damn it, I spent every minute of every waking day griping. For once in my life I was going to take action.

I surfed the internet until 3 am researching our Special Project. I pounced on Bertie the minute she arrived next morning and outlined my phased project approach: visualization, followed by planning, then implementation.

"Oh, come on," Bertie said, throwing off her coat. "You really have been a civil servant too long. Phased approach my ass – it's just your excuse to postpone implementation indefinitely."

"Well, I don't see anything wrong in sticking to Phase 1. Visioning Magda in the Iron Maiden really boosted my endorphins," I grumbled, though finishing off Ramona's truffles had helped, too.

"Medieval torture chambers? You are totally out to lunch." Bertie fired up her computer. "There!" A website on venomous snakes flared up on her screen. "Black or green mamba?"

I stared, staggered by the risk-benefit implications. "Now who's being unrealistic? Where the hell are we going to get a snake?"

"From Roger. He quit being Senior IT Manager last night. He and his partner are opening an exotic animal sanctuary."

But before we could work out the details, Magda called another staff meeting.

"You've all been sending me draft correspondence. This is unacceptable," she announced. "When your work reaches my desk, it must be pristine. Flawless. All 12 copies."

"12," Alicia, our Senior Policy Analyst, choked out.

"Yes, one for Dr. Nickle, one for his executive assistant, one for myself—" And she proceeded to list every manager in the Ministry who might have heard of our unit, and several more besides.

"Let me sketch out a little analogy. My country club doesn't just preach perfection," she went on. "The linen is crisp, the silver gleams. It's pure. Elegant. As your work should be. No drafts. Final version only. All I should have to do is sign."

With a wave of her hand, she dismissed us.

"She's insane," I bit out back at my desk. "Archives haven't accepted our hard copy files since we went electronic. We're drowning in paper." I pointed to the columns of dusty brown containers tottering toward the ceiling.

"So let's think outside the storage box – ha-ha!" Bertie leaned back in her worn chair. "Forget snakes for now. Let's be budget conscious and use the weapons at hand. I'll locate the key support boxes and do the math. Then we wait till Magda leaves her office, one quick push – and we *kill* her!"

"Yeah, right." I pulled a bulging file from my in-tray and logged in. But visioning Magda crushed to a pulp by her true love, paper, did give me the warm fuzzies for the rest of the day. That is, until Ramona handed me my Minister's letter and I learned that Magda loved mutating commas as much as Vlad the Spellchecker. 12 times over.

Work continued its death spiral. Every time Magda sent back a letter, Ramona had to produce 12 more copies. The Supernova insisted that all our draft copies be archived to track her revisions. Soon a towering cityscape of storage boxes eclipsed our cramped quarters. It broke my heart to see poor Ramona sobbing with frustration, seared by the harsh light of the Xerox machine or smeared with dust from heaving file boxes around.

Bertie's engineering calculations and drawings kept us going until the morning we met in the food court for a pre-work coffee and doughnut.

"We can't do it," she announced. "Ramona spends all her time next to those damn storage boxes. If we start our avalanche, we risk killing her as well."

"So we go back to snakes."

"Same collateral problem. Now it's your turn to think of something."

But my imagination had gone dry. That is, until that afternoon when Magda forced Ramona to collect donations for her brat's ballet recital. And her younger brat's art school benefit. Minimum 'suggested' donation $20. Each kid.

Grudgingly, Bertie and I coughed up to stay employed, and to cover Ramona's share since she didn't have an extra cent after paying her baby's day care fees. So good-bye to our blessed sanctuary, the food court, and the snacks therein.

The staff drew lots to see who would take the filled donation envelope back to Magda's office.

I lost.

The Supernova sat munching her carefully purified lunch of organic salad and imported spring water, as serene as the gleam on her mahogany desk. Her handsome husband, darling daughters and golden retriever beamed at me from the silver-framed photograph beside her.

She embraced me with her smile, pushed her salad to one side and said, "Lorraine, this is timely. Sit down over there with Alicia."

I hadn't seen Alicia come in. I dropped the envelope on her desk and, furious with my trembling legs, took the chair next to our respected Senior Policy Analyst.

Magda rested her firm chin on her hand and looked at each of us in turn. "I've been meaning to speak to you both," she said. "When one is – how shall I put it – mature, and of a certain size, it is even more vital to project a professional image."

"I *am* a professional," Alicia boomed.

I didn't share her courage. Pathetic defenses for being fat and 50 stormed through my brain. "But nobody sees us here," I blurted out. "Why shouldn't we be comfortable?"

"Looking professional nurtures productivity. It engenders a culture of effectiveness that shines through in your writing. Something that's lacking in both your work. So remedy this issue…I'm sure you understand."

A strange hissing noise filled my ears. Alicia was turning crimson, the whites of her eyes showing. I've never heard so many expletives so loudly delivered. And so creatively juxtaposed. Ten minutes later I stood gasping in the aftermath of Alicia's resignation.

Magda seemed strangely unperturbed. She picked up a Holt Renfrew bag from the floor. "Take these down to shoe repair, would you?"

"What, now?" I stammered.

"Yes, now. My husband and I are attending a reception for the Duke of Edinburgh tonight."

I lurched back to my desk, clutching that stupid bag. Bertie ran after me as I headed toward the elevators.

"We're going for a medicinal doughnut," she said, grabbing my arm. "Forget the money and the Supernova's ban on coffee breaks."

I was too stunned to argue, and, comforted by a strawberry cream special, I spilled out the details of the whole sordid, humiliating experience.

"That bitch! Give me those shoes!" Bertie yanked the bag from my lap and drew out a stiletto sandal with diamante straps. Seizing the metal knife beside her plate, she worked its edge into the gap between the heel and the silver sole. "Let's make sure she breaks her heel and her neck at her la-di-da reception."

"Stop! Are you crazy? The police will know we did it."

"All right, you win," Bertie tossed the shoe back at me. "At least Alicia's happy."

"But she quit!"

"Exactly. Did you know that Alicia used to be a research chemist? Her old professor wants her back at the university."

I shook my head. Lucky Alicia…then I had a terrible idea…

"Not bad," Bertie said after I explained it. "Alicia's professor *does* have loads of lovely poisons. We could get cyanide, potassium chloride, dioxin…"

"How about strychnine?"

"Nasty." Bertie grinned, showing her sharp white teeth. "About time you grew a spine." She swept away the crumbs from her apple fritter and picked up our used paper cups. "I'll get Alicia to show me her professor's lab tonight. Tomorrow we implement!"

That night I woke up with a beating heart. What the hell were we doing? Bertie wouldn't really steal the poison, would she? After all, our Special Project was just a joke, a harmless safety valve to stop us going crazy, wasn't it? Just like our boss-cataloguing system.

I staggered into my kitchenette, threw open the fridge door, and grabbed a cool metal can of diet Pepsi, holding it to my burning forehead. Even if Magda was the boss from hell, we didn't have the right to take her life. I thought of her handsome husband and her two little girls in the photo on her desk. And the dog. A dream family like the one I'd never have thanks to my cheating husband and the passage of time. It would all be better in the morning, I told myself. We just went a little off the rails…

Boy, was I wrong!

"See this?" Bertie said, dangling a Ziploc bag of white powder in my face. "Now we implement. No excuses."

"Bertie, this isn't a good time…"

"Sure it is. Magda's meeting with Vlad the Spellchecker. They'll be at it for hours. Time to spice up that pure organic salad she keeps in her mini-fridge for lunch."

"We-we can't do this."

"We'll draw lots."

Once again, I lost.

I swallowed and stared at that innocuous-looking white powder. "Bertie…"

"Did you notice that Ramona isn't here?"

I had, but I'd assumed she was hiding out in the washroom, her one refuge from the Supernova.

"Magda fired her this morning."

"But she's a union member!"

"Magda's connected. Even our union won't mess with Vlad's prodigy. Now are you going to do it?"

I sighed and nodded. Holding the plastic bag with my fingertips, I crept into Magda's office. Stared at the stainless steel mini-fridge that held the environmentally cleansed fixings of her lunch. Caught sight of that silver-framed family portrait…

"You coward!" Bertie declared as I slumped back down behind my desk.

"Please, let's forget it!"

"No way." She tore the plastic bag from my hand and shoved it into the pocket of her jacket. Eyes gleaming, she brushed back her spiky hair and tromped into Magda's office.

Oh, my God! She was really going to do it. I rested my forehead on my desk so I wouldn't have to look.

The elevator doors chimed open. Through the gap in the ratty cloth dividers of our cubicle, I spotted the Supernova heading straight for her office. She'd descended from Vlad's heavenly sphere early. This couldn't be happening!

I leapt up to warn Bertie. Too late! My ears were bombarded by Magda's ferocious shouts.

A melee of staff and security guards poured into her office. I dove into the crowd, using my sturdy hips to knock bodies out of the way. I struggled over to the spot where the guards were manhandling Bertie and snatched that dreadful envelope from where she'd dropped it on the floor.

Not that it helped. Magda kept shouting murder. The security guards marched Bertie over to the elevators and out the door. Someone shouted that a police car was waiting outside.

Bertie arrested? I couldn't move.

"You and your damn friend are pathetic," Magda cried as our eyes met. "You can't stop my reorganization. This unit is gone. And so are you. You don't deserve to be a professional. Go work in that precious food court of yours for minimum wage. If you're lucky enough to get hired."

In the quiet of the aftermath, I slipped into the washroom, and, in the inner sanctum of the stall, I flushed that damn envelope away. And with it, every grain of incriminating strychnine. Finally my tears came. Bertie was my best friend. She'd made my working life bearable. Now she wasn't just going to lose her home. She was going to go prison for years and years, because I hadn't tried hard enough to stop her.

And because of that hard-hearted bitch and her ridiculous penchant for purity.

As I crept out of the washroom, I spotted Magda in her wine-colored designer coat heading for the elevators. So she wasn't eating her organic salad at her desk today.

I watched her press the down button. So she was heading outside. Maybe even she needed to clear her head in the crisp spring air after this morning's drama.

The bones in my legs turned to steel. I ran after her, but her elevator doors closed in my face. I swore and jabbed the down button. An intense heat flooded through me. I could feel the give of her soft pearly throat under my powerful fingers.

By the time I reached the downstairs lobby, she was already outside, heading down the wide granite stairs to the sidewalk. Breathing hard, I chased after her. And caught up to her next to the scaffolding surrounding the half-demolished Archives Building

She seemed to sense me behind her. When she looked over her shoulder, her face went as pale as the 20-bond paper she adored. A strange power surged through me in rhythm with her fear. Never get Lorraine angry, people said. When she loses it—

A strange whistling wind charged towards us. A tremendous pendulum of steel swept past my arm.

And Magda's head vanished in an explosion of blood and brains.

I froze, gawping. One second she was our cold-hearted unit director, the next a mess on the sidewalk. I'd never seen anyone die before. I couldn't breathe. For the second time that day, I was submerged in a crowd of shouting people.

***

The paramedics couldn't do anything for Magda, but they dragged me off to the hospital where the docs downgraded my 'heart attack' to a stress reaction. Bertie fought her way past the nurses to find me.

"Bertie, thank God!" I cried. "I thought the police arrested you."

"For what? Alicia didn't put strychnine in the bag. She gave me a powerful laxative to give Magda a wake-up call, but you – you bloody genius!" She plopped an armload of red roses into my lap. "Everyone at work got together and bought you these."

I didn't know what to say. In dull moments, I liked to pretend I had superpowers, but, of course, I hadn't killed Magda. A renegade steel beam from the crumbling Archives Building had crashed through the construction barrier and done that.

"Guess what?" Bertie went on. "My lawyer says old Vlad wants to settle. He's terrified of more bad publicity since Magda's 'accident'. So let's take my exit package and open a chocolate shop together. I'm serious. Think about it."

I did, during my endless first morning back at work with only my food court snack for company. Everyone who hadn't already quit our unit had called in sick.

"Ms., um, Fraser, is it?" asked a raspy voice.

I nearly choked on my maple-cream doughnut. Vlad the Spellchecker himself had materialized in front of my desk! Greasy fronds of greying hair hung over his spotty scalp. His dry, thin-skinned hands clutched Magda's familiar Holt Renfrew bag.

"Glad to see that you, ah, are feeling better in time for Ms. Molina's memorial service."

So that's why everyone had stayed away from the office today. They might have told me!

"Get your coat, there's a good girl. My driver will take us."

If only I'd had a wooden stake handy!

As it turned out, we got stuck in the heavy downtown traffic, leaving me free to stare at the chunks of dandruff adorning Vlad's black suit while he fumbled through the Holt

Renfrew bag, muttering to himself. I gathered that his assistant had got the address wrong and that we were seriously late.

We finally pulled up outside a low stone church that we'd passed three times already. We raced up the flagstone path to find it completely deserted except for a trim elderly lady in an elegant navy suit.

"I'm terribly sorry. The service is over," she told us.

Vlad had the good grace to look embarrassed as he gave her our names.

"Dr. Nickle, yes, of course. You were Magda's mentor," the lady said. "I'm Iris McKenzie. And Lorraine, you're the one who saw—"

I nodded and choked up. Iris had to be Magda's mother-in-law.

"Let's sit down," she said with capable calm, indicating the pew beside her. "Magda talked so much about all of you at the Ministry. I feel as if I know you already."

That made me squirm. "There must have been quite a crowd at the service," I said.

"Really, dear, do you see anyone here?"

So Magda had put off her society friends, too. How awful her family must have felt when no one bothered to turn up. No wonder they'd left already. My breathing grew shorter just thinking about them. Perhaps it was a blessing we were late. What would I have said to her husband? To her little girls? That I had wanted to kill their mother?

"Poor Magda, she should have taken more interest in life," Iris sighed.

Old Vlad stiffened at that. "She was a superb manager, a brilliant communicator," he intoned.

"Work was her life," Iris agreed. "But a poor substitute for a real one."

But she did have a life, I thought. She had her perfect family, a gorgeous house and brilliant society parties. Vlad uttered a dusty cough, reached into the Holt Renfrew bag, and pulled out Magda's silver-framed family portrait. "Under the circumstances, I should like to, ah, return this."

Iris gasped and took it from him. "Where did you find this?"

"Magda had it on her desk at work," I said.

"Oh, heavens, that poor misguided woman! This is my favorite photo of my son and his children."

"But-but wasn't Magda your daughter-in-law?" I stammered.

"Oh, dear me, no, Magda and I weren't related. She just rented my coach house. My son lives with his family in Australia. That poor girl didn't have anyone in the world!"

***

Back outside old Vlad looked like he'd been scorched by the rising sun. "I confess, Ms. Fraser that I don't fully understand—"

"I do," I burst out. "Magda wanted a family so desperately, she stole Iris's. Her glorious private life was nothing but an elaborate lie!"

Vlad winced. "There must be some mistake."

"The mistake Magda made was devoting her life to chasing idiotic edits in useless documents. Just like I've been doing for 20 years."

"Calm yourself, Ms. Fraser. And I shouldn't have to remind you to keep this little incident confidential..."

If I'd been a Comet, I would have used Magda's secret to worm myself into a promotion back at Vlad's moldy ministry. Instead I turned my back on the old bugger and left him standing open-mouthed next to his long dark limo.

So here I am charging down the twisting streets of Rosedale. Forget the bus or the subway. I'm walking the six miles to Bertie's house, where I'm going to get down on my hands and knees and beg her to open our chocolate shop.

So what if I'm 50? It's time I had a real life.

THE DOG ON BALMY BEACH

I wrote this story based on a news report about a young man who'd planned to carry out a mass shooting on the boardwalk in the Toronto Beaches District. Especially chilling because my friends and I walk and bike there regularly.

Published in Going Out With a Bang, Anthology *by the Ladies Killing Circle, Rendezvous Crime / Dundurn Press, 2008.*

"My life is over," Ora said to the sky, the sand and the implacable blue lake before her.

Melanie, content on the hard wooden bench beside her, ran her swollen, misshapen fingers through her guide dog's golden fur. As always, she didn't acknowledge Ora's heartfelt declaration.

Sometimes I wonder why we're still friends, Ora thought. *Nothing's changed since our teacher put us at the same reading table in Grade One. After 55 years, can't she sense that I'm desperate to talk to someone? Especially today.*

Melanie leaned down, touching Basil's nose with her own. "You want pet mode, don't you, boy?" His feathery tail thumped on the boardwalk. She fumbled with the metal clasps of the dog's harness while he struggled to be free.

"That is a really bad idea," Ora said.

"Basil needs to run off his spring friskies." Melanie's mouth curved in a mischievous smile. "He already got away from me once this morning."

A nightmare image flashed into Ora's mind of the big golden retriever plunging in front of the Queen Streetcar dragging Melanie with him. She made a grab for Basil's harness, but he slipped free, bounding onto the wide stretch of silver beach before them.

"Relax for once. He'll be fine." Melanie turned her broad face to the pale morning sun and folded her hands over her worn beige parka. "And you'll find another job. You're a survivor."

No, I won't, Ora wanted to scream. Melanie floated through life oblivious to its malicious blows, even to the multiple sclerosis that had stolen her sight. But then she'd never really had to worry about anything. Her disability pension covered her modest needs. And her friends always leaped forward to care for her whenever she had a crisis.

No one does that for me, Ora thought pulling her red cashmere coat tighter against the biting wind. *I can't get up again, not this time.*

"Come on, they'd be crazy not to hire you," Melanie said. "You're so organized."

Oh, yes, I'm very organized, Ora thought. She felt in her pocket to make sure the bottle of pills was still there. She'd set everything out on the dining room table back at her condo: her list of instructions, cash to cover the costs, her best black dress...

"Aren't you curious to know how I got Basil back?" Melanie asked, startling Ora back to reality.

The dog had reached the water's edge. He ran back and forth full of energy.

"All right, I'm listening," Ora said. Basil remained immune to entreaties, toys and food whenever she tried them.

22

"A nice young man helped me. He startled me in the first place – that was the problem. He came rushing out of those bushes up by the reservoir. I tripped, dropped Basil's harness and off he went."

"You shouldn't walk on the beach when nobody's around," Ora said. These days only dark human motives occurred to her.

"Oh, come on. Anyway I figured Basil would head for the lake just to be a bugger. I kind of staggered off the boardwalk, so the man said sorry, he didn't see I was blind and he'd fetch Basil. 'Hope you like swimming,' I told him. And he said, 'Your dog won't go in. The water's too cold.' So I said, 'Forget that. Basil thinks he's part polar bear.'"

Ora watched Melanie's polar bear leap at a seagull and fortunately miss. "So Basil rewarded him with a soak."

"Not exactly." Melanie chuckled. "When the guy brought Basil back, he asked me why nobody was on the boardwalk today. Obviously he wasn't a Beacher or he'd know that only dog walkers are nutty enough to brave the lake on a cold spring day like this one."

"And *that* didn't make you feel scared?"

"Honestly, I don't know how you can go through life being so paranoid."

A loud noise burst through the pale quiet.

"What was that?" Ora sprang up. She looked up and down the boardwalk, but spotted no one. "That sounded like a gunshot."

"Relax, it's just kids with firecrackers."

But it's not Victoria Day yet, Ora thought. She gazed at the shoreline. Basil had dwindled to a tiny yellow dot amidst the silvery driftwood and white specks of gulls. Time to drag him back, if she could manage to catch him. She studied her impractical black business pumps. How to navigate the sand in these?

"*Look out!*" an arrogant voice shouted next to her ear.

A hard blow to her shoulder sent her staggering. A man on roller blades shot past. She had a brief glimpse of a straggling grey ponytail and knotted veins in muscular calves.

"Bastard," she managed, brushing off her coat. Seething, she watched him stride away over the rough boards, heading east toward the reservoir.

"I'll bet that was Tyrone, the old hippy," Melanie said from the bench. "Grey hair? Frisbee?"

"Yes," Ora bit out. She resumed her seat next to her friend and tugged her coat even tighter.

"He blades here every morning, hoping to find young boys."

"How do you know that?"

"The other dog walkers told me." Melanie smiled, pulled off her brown knitted hat and shook out her grey braids. "They say he skates up and down the boardwalk because the school banned him from hanging around the playground. Even his own wife kicked him out."

"Wonderful! So he's a pervert as well as very rude." Ora squinted into the sun. Tyrone had shrunk to a small black dot in the distance.

"Forget Tyrone. You didn't hear the end of my story. Basil let the young man catch him, but he got his revenge."

Ora stiffened. "What did Basil do?"

"The guy shouts, 'Your dog's got his face in my pack.' So I said. 'Did you have food in there?' And he said, 'Yeah, a sandwich.' 'You don't any more,' I said. 'But it was wrapped in plastic,' the poor guy says. Honest to God, I couldn't help laughing. 'That won't stop Basil,' I told him 'but it'll sure explain his weird poop and scoop tonight.'"

"Oh, for heaven's sake. You should have paid the man for his sandwich."

Melanie shrugged. "By the time I got Basil's harness back on, he'd left."

"Where did he go?"

Another burst of firecrackers made Ora jump. Shielding her eyes, she failed to pinpoint the source of the sound.

Melanie fiddled with her braids. "I missed you at the poetry reading last week."

"Sorry." *At least after today I won't have to sit through another evening of suffocating feminist poetry,* Ora thought.

At the far end of the boardwalk where the path climbed up to the filtration plant, the dark outline of the man appeared. He was carrying a bulky pack by the shoulder straps.

And he was coming towards them.

"Let's go back to Queen Street for a coffee," Ora said, suddenly nervous.

"Can't you stop twitching? Where's Basil?"

Now Basil, too, had vanished. Ora shouted the dog's name. No sign of him.

Where is he?

The man drew closer. He was wearing heavy black boots like the ones skinheads favored. He looked like a skinhead, too, with his closely shaved head and baggy camouflage pants. Ora's skin prickled as if it were full of tiny electric needles, the way it did whenever she had a near miss in traffic. Or last week when her new boss asked her into his office and closed the door.

Suddenly Basil came hurtling out of nowhere, a gold cannonball. Where had he been? He flew past Ora to Melanie who stroked and tussled his fur. "You're all wet, boy. What have you been doing?"

"For God's sake, Melanie, hold him." A dark oily substance clung to the dog's chest and forelegs. "He's got blood on him!" she cried. "It's all over your hands."

"Oh, my God, is he hurt?"

"Basil, stay still." Ora pulled out the small plastic packet of tissues she always carried in her pocket and tried to wipe him off. In an instant, the papers were soaked a dark reddish brown, but with intense relief, she spotted no wounds. "He's fine. He hasn't cut himself. Here, give me your hands." She used the remaining tissues to clean her friend's fists, one at a time.

"Bad dog, where have you been?" Ora went on, glaring at Basil who bounced out of her reach. "Rolling on a filthy, dead sea gull, I bet. And what have you got in your mouth?"

Basil tried to dodge her, but this time she was able to snatch the red disk free of his teeth. It was a faded Frisbee, pock-marked with threadlike tufts of worn plastic. Dark fluid had settled under the rim, streaking her hands as well.

Horrible, Ora thought. *How could the bird's blood end up there?* She chucked the toy onto the sand. Basil leapt down and scooped it up instantly. "Bad dog," she told him while she foraged through her purse, looking for a bit of paper, anything, to clean her fingers. She settled on her check book, tearing off the numbered pages, crumpling and tossing them to the wind, one by one, as she used them. No value to me anymore, she thought.

Finished, she looked up. Her heart beat faster.

The man stood 15 feet away. Motionless, he stared across the lake, his heavy shoulders turned slightly away from them. He dropped his pack on the boards. Ora felt the vibration through the thin soles of her shoes.

Basil bounded up to man, tail wagging. He nudged the man's leg and dropped the Frisbee beside him. The man's large fist hung down, unresponsive. The dog nudged him again.

"Bad dog," Ora called out. "Come here, Basil. Bad dog."

The man leaned down and picked up the toy. He stared at Ora. Smiled as he sensed her fear. With a sweep of his muscled arm, he flung the Frisbee out over the sand. Basil shot after it.

"Basil!" Ora sprang up. The dog caught the Frisbee in a white flash of teeth. He galloped over the beach, running around and around in a great circle, tail raised to the sky. "Here, boy. Come here, good dog."

Ignoring her pleas, he headed straight back to the man who, with a coolly contemptuous glance at the two women, tossed the Frisbee again.

"For heaven's sake," Ora said. "Melanie, help me for once. Call your dog. He never comes to me."

"What's the big rush?"

"It's some man. He looks like a skinhead. He's using that mucky toy to play fetch with Basil."

"So let them play."

"Melanie…" Ora tried to rein in her voice. Her new boss had accused her of being loud and shrill. "I want to leave. He's making me nervous."

"Oh, stop it. Why do we always have to do what you want? You haven't changed since grade school."

"And you've never grown out of grade school," Ora flared. "You only survive because your friends and I look out for you. And who looks out for me? Nobody!"

"Why does it always have to be about you?" A dark obstinacy twisted Melanie's mouth. "If you're that worried, go home. I'm staying till Basil gets tired."

Anger charged Ora's courage. She crossed over the worn brown planks of the boardwalk until she was within striking distance of the man. He was scribbling in a notebook clipped to his belt by a thin brass chain. She realized that he was young, no more than 25. In spite of the cold, he wore only a drab green singlet over his pants. Her new boss like to call those tank tops "wife beater shirts", no doubt to fool his staff into believing that he was young, modern and full of ideas. He liked to show off his tattoo on casual Fridays, too, but his discreet Zen symbol looked laughably puny next to the vivid, diabolical patterns that swirled up the forearms of Basil's new friend.

Basil had returned, his pink tongue spilling blissfully from his mouth, the Frisbee an offering at the stranger's feet. The man looked up from his notebook.

She gasped. Cobra eyes, red diamonds on a yellow background, bored down on her. Contact lenses, she realized, recovering. She'd spotted similar ones in the window of a "Goth shop" that she'd passed on her way to a gallery opening on Queen Street West.

He dropped his notebook. It swung on its chain as his arm flicked out, hurling the Frisbee. Basil charged after it.

Ora's knees wavered. A metal tube with an oily blue sheen protruded through the top of his pack. *Oh, God, he has a gun.*

Heart pounding, she cleared her throat. *Pretend everything's normal.* "Excuse me, are you the man who helped my friend get her dog back?" she asked. The man ignored her. "If you are, my friend's sorry about your sandwich. I – I mean *we* – want to pay you for it."

28

"Doesn't your friend feed her dog?"

So it is him. Words rushed into her dry throat. "Of course Melanie feeds him, but Basil has an uncontrollable passion for bread. Today in the bakery cafe, it was so funny..." she pushed her fingers against her mouth to force the tremor out of her voice, "Basil stole four croissants when the owner wasn't looking. The minute her back was turned, up he went on his hind legs and plucked them delicately off the counter. She turned around, he ate one. She turned around, he ate another. Basil moves like lightning. He's quite graceful for such a big dog."

"And you didn't stop him. Just sat there and laughed," he broke in.

Ora blinked. "I paid the bakery back, of course."

"That's what you rich bitches do. Pay people off."

"I'm not rich, I'm broke." The words erupted, anger and humiliation overriding her fear. "The bank fired me last week after 25 years." *And I listened to investment advice from my cheating, incompetent ex-husband.*

"Oh, boo-hoo." He jerked the rifle from his pack. A military model with a mounted telescope sight. He braced it on his shoulder and scanned the horizon, squinting through the lens.

Act normal, just act normal. "Look here, I know it's none of my business, but isn't what you're doing illegal?"

"You're right. It's none of your business."

It's OK, she told herself. *That old hippy Tyrone skates up and down the boardwalk. He'll be back any minute. He can help us, even if he is a pervert.*

The barrel of the rifle swept back and forth along the water line. *Where was Basil?*

"Please put that away. You could hurt the dog—"

The roar of the rifle cut through her words. In the distance, a rupture of white feathers. Gulls shrieked, swirling in a mad white tornado. Their noise was intense, terrifying.

Basil! Where's Basil? To Ora's overwhelming relief, the dog stood frozen, tail down, halfway to the water.

"Ora?" Melanie cried back at the bench. "Where's Basil?"

"Playing."

"What's going on?"

"Nothing is going on," Ora bit out. Summoning every authoritative instinct she'd honed on the job, she brushed past the man and stepped down off the boardwalk. Cold sand poured into her shoes. She stumbled over fragments of bone-white shell, rusted bits of metal, and crumbles of Styrofoam, the urban detritus of a harsh winter, trying to keep the dog in sight. With every step, she felt the man's crimson cobra eye through the gun sight, burying into her spine. *Move, move,* she urged her legs.

She'd only covered a few feet when a piercing whistle drilled through the air. Basil trotted obediently over to the man who lowered his rifle. A sharp click. He appeared to be reloading.

By the time Ora had staggered back to Melanie's bench, Melanie had wavered to her feet, the dog's harness jingling in her hand. Ora seized her friend's arm and said in loud whisper, "Try not to react. He has a gun."

"What? Why is he shooting?"

"He's killing sea gulls. For now."

"What?!" Melanie's podgy features spasmed.

"Listen to me! Get Basil over here and harness him up. I'll keep the guy talking. Hopefully, he'll think I'm a nattering, useless old woman like everybody else does. Haul your butt back up to Queen Street. Call the police."

"What?"

"Call your dog!"

"Ora!" Melanie's fists clutched her coat. "Don't leave me."

Ora broke free. Teetering on her heels, she forced herself back over to the stranger.

Watching the man's muscles flex under his thin shirt as he stared down the rifle barrel, she feared her bladder would give way. She was thin, suffering from the beginnings of osteoporosis. Physically she didn't stand a chance. She waved madly at Basil, willing him to return to Melanie, but the dog uttered a low whine, crept forward, and nuzzled the man's knee. The man rested his free hand on the dog's forehead.

"Basil likes you," she managed to say.

The man ran a finger over Basil's head. The dog's deep brown eyes studied him as if he were the only human left in the world. The man lowered the gun, picked up the Frisbee. He tossed it in the direction of the seagulls. Basil shot after it. In an instant, the rifle flew back to his shoulder.

"For God's sake, what are you doing?" Ora screamed. Instinctively, her hands clawed the man's hard arm to grab the gun. A toss of his shoulder sent her reeling.

"Fuck you, lady."

"And fuck you right back. How can you shoot an innocent animal? He trusts you, you damn coward!"

Turning, he fired. The cloud of gulls erupted. Basil, unharmed, dashed into the whirlwind of feathers. He chased the maddened birds, his barks echoing.

"I wasn't shooting at the dog," the man said, with a murderous look at Ora. He opened and closed the rifle with icy precision.

"Why are you shooting the birds? They have a right to live."

"I'm purging the world of vermin."

"That was you shooting earlier, wasn't it?"

He shoved the rifle under his arm, grabbed his notebook, and began writing. Back at the bench, Melanie slumped over, sobbing.

"You've upset my friend," Ora said, her fear burning away. "She thinks you shot her dog. He's not just her pet, you know. He's her life."

No response. He kept on writing.

"The Lions Club didn't want Melanie to have him, because Basil is, well, unfocused, that's how they put it. They were going to put him down. They'd just lost $25,000 and two years training him. But Melanie was so attached to him, I talked to my contact there, my former brother-in-law..."

"Shut up, lady. I know what you're doing."

"Oh," Ora stammered. "What am I doing?" She waited a moment. When he didn't reply, she said, "You're right, I'm not good at establishing rapport. I can't talk people into anything. Or out of anything. In meetings, I can't spell out what everyone's thinking. Or should be thinking. My brain doesn't work that way."

"Your brain doesn't work at all."

"My ex-boss would agree with you."

"You don't know who I am."

"Yes, I do." She hesitated then said, "I was waiting for you last night. And this morning."

He raised an eyebrow.

"You're Death."

"You're full of shit. You're pathetic thinking you can trick me by acting all spiritual and New Age."

"I am not full of shit." Ora wrenched the pills from her coat pocket. "See these?"

"Tylenol," he snorted.

"Barbiturates. I was going to down them with a pint of vodka and get into the Jacuzzi. The hot water opens your veins, makes the drug absorb faster. But I couldn't do it. I just couldn't."

"You're just whining because you're broke."

"You're young. You don't know what it means to lose your savings at my age. If only I'd been able to keep on working." The words cascaded out, Ora couldn't stop them. "So stupid to carry on like I was still 35. Your abilities fade. Everyone knows it but you. And you learn that life has limits. The story ends. So much sooner than I ever thought possible."

Basil came loping back across the stretch of sand. He edged closer to the man and dropped the Frisbee, panting expectantly. The man dropped his notebook and fondled the dog's head with his free hand, ruffling his ears, rubbing his chin.

"Life is a box, lady."

"I can't disagree with you."

Ora's legs trembled so violently, she collapsed and sat down on the boardwalk, dangling her legs over the edge. She tipped the sand out of one shoe, then the other. Melanie uttered a low keening wail, curled sideways on her bench. *She can't even save herself,* Ora thought in desperate frustration.

"What has made you so angry?" she asked the man.

"Stop the social worker shit." He forced the rifle back together. "Don't pretend you never wanted to blow someone to pieces."

"I did want my ex-boss to die with all my heart." She relived the patronizing, dismissive words he'd dispensed at their last meeting. They'd burned away the last illusion of her self-worth like acid.

The dog settled between them, resting his chin on the man's black boot. Ora curled a hand around Basil's leather collar. She swallowed and said, "You shouldn't give up in spite of what I'm planning to do. I'm old, I've run out of time. But you're young, you have decades to reclaim your life."

"No," he said with quiet finality. "I shot somebody."

She knew then that Tyrone wasn't coming back. And that Basil's joyous new dog toy must be Tyrone's Frisbee, soaked in the old hippy's blood.

"You shot Tyrone, the old hippy, didn't you? Out on the reservoir where the boardwalk ends."

His eyes narrowed. His bones seemed to harden as she watched.

"Did Tyrone collide with you? Is that what happened? Or was he just in the wrong place at the wrong time?"

"I was waiting for him."

"What?"

"He was my father."

A cry of horrified surprise escaped her. "He abused you."

"*Shut up!*" His fists looked like they'd break his gun apart.

"Ora!" Melanie sobbed. "Where's Basil? Tell me he's all right."

"Make her shut the fuck up."

Ora stood up, grasping Basil up by his collar. "I'll take Melanie home. We'll leave you alone."

"Go sit on the bench. The dog stays."

"My friend needs her dog."

"*The dog stays.*"

His rifle was pointing directly at her face, inches from her chin. She stared into the two black pitiless holes in disbelief. Death, even though she'd longed for it, still astonished her.

"Are you deaf? Go sit on the bench."

"What are you going to do?" Ora asked, though she knew very well.

"Don't you ever stop talking?" he asked wearily. Ora released her grip on Basil's collar and backed away from him.

"Wait!"

She froze in her tracks.

"You're old. You'd know. He's dead, but he's still in my head. How long before he goes away?"

"Your mind is keeping Tyrone alive." She thought of her ex-boss. She'd let his odious words destroy her spirit, had nearly let them kill her. And now when she knew that only she could save herself, it was too late. "Your hatred is too strong. He'll never leave unless you get help."

"Fuck you."

"I know it isn't what you wanted me to say, but please, don't do this."

"Forget it, lady."

"Shoot me if you want, but please don't hurt my friend." To her shame and dismay, tears streaked down her cheeks, dribbling off her chin. "My friend has never hurt anyone in her life. All she wants is to write bad poetry and live out her life with Basil. Please, I'm begging you, leave her alone."

"Go sit on the bench."

Ora dropped onto the seat next to Melanie, her limbs numb. "What's happening, Ora?" Melanie whimpered. "What is he going to do? I can't hear Basil."

"Basil's fine. Everything is going to be all right."

Melanie wiped her eyes. "I should have listened to you. And not just today. I'm sorry, Ora."

"Don't apologize. Everything is absolutely fine." She reached over and gripped her friend's hand tightly.

She felt Basil brush past her leg. He padded over next to Melanie, sighed and sat down. Sobbing, Melanie plunged her hands in his fur.

Ora heard the man's heavy boots on the boardwalk, then a dull clump as he stepped off into the soft earth beside it. *He's going behind us. He's going to do it from behind.*

She closed her eyes. Waited.

Why is he taking so long? Why doesn't he just do it?

We're all together, she thought. *It'll all be over in the wink of an eye. We're here and in the next instant, we won't be. Here and not here. Here and not here,* she chanted silently.

The explosion, when it came, was the loudest sound Ora had ever heard. Light burst into her eyes. Melanie clutched her arm so painfully she cried out.

She felt icy cold, but she could still see. She could still breathe. Slowly, the sounds of the world seeped back: the clang of the streetcar across Kew Gardens, the whistling of wind from the lake, Melanie's deep sobs, Basil's frenzied barking...

The back of Melanie's parka was peppered with red dots. Her own hair was wet from a soft scarlet rain. She turned to look behind them.

"What's happened?" Melanie choked out.

Ora stifled a ridiculous warning not to look. "Hold onto Basil," she said.

She staggered, stumbling down off the boards onto the grass to kneel next to the crimson nightmare behind their bench. His notebook had fallen open, its stained pages rustling in the wind.

She couldn't help herself. Her fingers reached for the brass chain and pulled the book over. Heart pounding, she took the edge of the last page. Made out the words 'dog' and 'soul'. Underneath he'd scrawled, 'Dog needs blind lady. Only way.'

She bent her head and cried.

THE WIDOWS AND ORPHANS FUND

I began this story began after seeing a beautiful stained glass window portraying the Archangel, St. Michael. And asking what if gender issues were punished like crimes?

Published in Futures Mystery Anthology Magazine, *March, 2007*

"What if everything anyone ever told you was a lie?
What if witches were good and water ran uphill?
What if you were innocent?"

"I got another one of those stupid letters," Edith said, shoving the crumpled paper into her young social worker's face. "Why is this person pestering me?"

Robin sighed. "Edith, try to find the positive. The person who wrote that poem must care about you."

Even the grey granular prison light couldn't dim Robin's fresh complexion. For a moment Edith hated her. "If they care so much, why don't they have the guts to sign their name?"

"Perhaps they're shy." Robin's dark eyes shone with the assurance of theoretical knowledge.

"Well, I am *not* innocent." Edith screwed the note into a ball, tossed it on the floor and watched it bounce. The letters contained nothing but the same poem, over and over, written on candy pink stationery as thick as blotting paper.

"Let's focus on launching your new life."

"A string of minimum wage jobs until I'm old enough to collect old age security and live on cat food? I can't wait."

"But at WOF you'll explore many opportunities—"

"WOF? It sounds like a dog."

"WOF stands for Work, Outreach and Fulfilment. Ava Flood asked for you personally for her 'Miracles' pilot."

"I want a real half-way house."

"Ava specializes in healing trauma."

"I told you before — I don't want to go on parole."

Wearily Robin retrieved the pink note, smoothed it out and tucked it into her file folder. "Edith, being 45 isn't the end of the world. You can still grow as a person."

Boy, platitudes poured from her as furiously as the stale air rattling through the ventilation system above their heads, Edith thought.

"Besides non-violent offenders are routinely paroled," Robin added.

Non-violent? Don't be too sure.

In the end though Edith gave in. She had no choice. She never did. At times, she felt that other people surrounded her like mountains. She crouched in their shadows while they made the decisions, her life a pathetic path through a gallery of institutions — school, church, Shipmaster Financial, prison. But, she conceded, parole did represent an opportunity.

An opportunity to see Paul again.

But, as usual, wistful fantasy and the real world diverged completely. WOF didn't turn out to be a modern facility in the downtown core. It occupied a somber historical mansion next to a park in a respectable residential area. No sign identified it. Its blood-red sandstone façade possessed the same aura of invisibility as Paul's exclusive men's club where they'd had their first lunch together. Probably why the well-off, law-abiding neighbors allowed WOF to exist.

Edith couldn't resist bumping Robin with her battered back-pack as they climbed the stone stairs to WOF's gothic doorway. When they passed through the revolving glass door, she took careful note of the gravel paths criss-crossing the park, the row of shops on the far side and the bus stop on the corner.

Soon, she reassured herself. *Soon.*

In the lobby a stained glass window scattered jewels of ruby, blue and emerald on the polished parquet floor. She gazed up at the image of a beautiful man astride a white horse. His skin was pale milk, his long hair gold, his sword a shimmering arc of silver as he rode down the demons of Hell.

"That's St. Michael, WOF's patron," Robin whispered reverently.

Edith blinked. "Is this place an old church?"

"No, Ava just likes St. Michael."

Odd thing Number One. Down the marble staircase came odd thing Number Two, a small, grey-haired African woman dressed in a severe navy-blue dress with white collar and cuffs. Robin introduced her as Aruba McCurdy, WOF's administrator. The Great Ava Flood was apparently too grand to be involved in daily operations.

McCurdy rolled out WOF's party line in a rich Scottish burr while Robin echoed her catch phrases with bright, manufactured enthusiasm. The Flood Methodology offered Nirvana to those who overhauled their attitudinal dysfunction. Books, exercises, and spiritual contemplation began this arduous process, but...

"What are you staring at?" McCurdy demanded in mid-stream.

"You're-you're not what I expected," Edith stammered.

"No." The older woman's eyes narrowed. "I have the blood of Zulu warriors and Scottish chieftains flowing through my veins. Can you say the same?"

"Well, um, no."

"I'll show you to your room."

McCurdy mounted the stairs at a brisk pace with Robin at her side. Edith trailed after them to the second floor. There she was confronted by Ava Flood's self-glorifying memorabilia everywhere she looked. Ava in formal portraits and in amateurish creations from grateful clients. Ava in a succession of photos with politicians and celebrities. Ava beaming from brochures and books strategically placed to catch the eye.

Please let there be something else to read, Edith prayed, but a stack of Ava's self-help tomes lurked on the nightstand beside the narrow bed in her tiny attic room. Worse, she was sandwiched between McCurdy on one side and Robin on the other. And they all shared the same ancient bathroom. Warfare seemed imminent.

"Why do *you* live here?" Edith asked Robin, not caring about being rude.

"Ava invited me after my, um, accident at the half-way house."

"Robin is very special to WOF," McCurdy intoned. "As am I."

I'm sure, Edith thought, tossing her backpack onto her bed. The minute their backs were turned, she'd be out that revolving door and gone for good. Mind you, she had no money and in truth, no place to go. No family, no friends.

Nothing but Paul. Or rather the memory of Paul.

But things will change.

Life at WOF began next morning and made Edith long for jail. There she'd had a modicum of privacy, but here her every move was scrutinized and remarked upon. Breakfast was at 8:25 am, not 8:24 or 8:26. McCurdy scanned the bathroom after she used it, a vengeful hawk on the look-out for dripping taps, specks of dirt in the sink or unreplenished toilet paper rolls. She hovered by Edith's shoulder, escorting her from the basement cafeteria to the morning's excruciating seminar – "Mining Your Life's Gold" — and back again. Afternoon mirrored morning except for the seminar title – "The Crystal Path to Miracles". No matter what Ava's aphorisms were quoted like gospel.

In the evening, back from her job, Robin took over from McCurdy, praising WOF's moist, mushy dinner, chiding Edith for her lack of appetite.

"Where is my parole card?" Edith cracked her tray against Robin's. "Why can't I make a move without McCurdy? When do I get out of here?" She'd quickly discovered that the revolving door was secured by metal bolts sunk into the floor.

Robin's smooth forehead puckered ever so slightly. "Ava believes in a phased approach to freedom."

Escape dominated Edith's every thought.

She ruled out a night-time flight. Only she, McCurdy and Robin slept at WOF and the two snakes remained vigilant, charging out of their bedrooms to check on her when she made a sound louder than a breath. During the day only a scattering of outsiders attended WOF's insipid seminars, so she'd be spotted immediately if she tried to slip away with them.

Next day she surfaced from the torrent of words erupting from the seminar leader. Raising her hand, she feigned a leaky bladder problem and was excused.

The air in WOF's lobby lay cool, fresh and still. McCurdy was nowhere to be seen. *Now what?* Looking down, she spotted a muscular young man with long dark hair bounding up WOF's stone steps. A bike courier.

Without further thought, she raced down the stairs to the lobby. When she reached the revolving door, she heard a loud click. The courier pushed in through one side while she pushed out the other. As she passed him, he threw her a saucy wink through the glass.

Ignoring him, she plunged into the park. She slumped down on a bench near a stone fountain. Irritably, she fluffed out her thin auburn hair with her fingers. She knew better than anyone that good-looking men only toyed with homely women. And she was homely. She'd been saddled with her father's prominent nose and chin – acceptable in an eccentric math professor perhaps but not in the daughter her socialite mother had wished for. Nor had her gift for numbers gained her a happy life.

A used paper cup lay squashed on the ground. Instinctively she picked it up. What was she thinking, running away from WOF with no money? She didn't even have change for a cup of coffee.

She turned the cup in her hands and let her thoughts stray to Paul. Funny how even his memory eluded her now. In her mind only fragments — his dark wavy hair, his easy smile, his taut skin.

Like that cheeky bike courier.

A sudden movement startled her. A coin dropped into the coffee cup. The bike courier stood astride his bike in front of her, laughing. With a cry of rage, she leapt to her feet, but he pedaled away, well out of her reach.

She collapsed back down onto the bench, tears of self-pity stinging her eyes. She *did* look like a bag lady with her rumpled, shapeless clothes and pasty skin. Another coin clinked in her cup, this time from a mother with her baby. She wiped her eyes and stared into the cup. Money at last.

On the other side of the park she discovered an internet café named The Cyber Warrior. Its sour coffee rivalled WOF's, but the banks of computer monitors made her fingers tingle. In prison, for the first time in her life, she'd had respect. She could tease goodies off the web with an ease even the toughest female inmates had admired. No money for a password today, but tomorrow...

Outside in the street, she ran smack into McCurdy and Robin.

"Edith, I'm so disappointed in you," the social worker said. "McCurdy had to call me at work."

"That bike courier ratted on me."

"Yes, Louis did his job." McCurdy folded her arms. "I knew you were a sneak the moment I laid eyes on you. The group leader tells me you're not doing your readings or indeed working at all." She drew herself up, with a great intake of breath. "Mrs. Flood is very concerned."

"Ava Bloody Flood doesn't know I'm alive. I bet she just exists on the covers of her boring books."

"Nonsense! She wants to see you. Right away, too."

Edith sized up the situation. She could outrun the old bat, but not Robin so she let them herd her back to WOF and up to the second floor.

McCurdy threw open a heavy, panelled door. "Here she is, Mrs. Flood."

"Leave us, McCurdy," said a prim voice flavoured with a faint European accent.

Edith entered the large office alone.

Ava Flood existed all right. And she confronted the world head-on with a carapace of fine grooming. Her pink suit – identical to the one in the oversized portrait above her head – molded her full figure. Though her bio put her at well over 50, her skin was as smooth and unlined as a doll's.

Ava studied Edith for a silent moment from where she sat behind her ivory and gilt desk. "McCurdy tells me you do not care for my books," she said.

"Meaningless New Age fluff," Edith snorted. "Overwritten and trite. I bet every one of your real-life stories is a lie."

"Amazing. You can't utter one nice word even out of courtesy. Why would anyone wish to remain as you are?"

"I feel just peachy."

"Do you know what happens to parolees who refuse to complete WOF's 'Miracles Pilot'?"

"Fine, ship me back to jail. Then I can read what I want!"

"You *are* a challenge." Ava tapped dangerously long fingernails on her desk. "Very well, McCurdy is overworked. You will help her with our accounts."

"I can't be an accountant anymore."

"Take your negative energy out of here." Ava waved a hand. "I advise you to cooperate."

That evening, Edith couldn't help smiling in spite of the boiled mess on her dinner plate. Office work meant computers and computers meant access to the Internet.

But again, WOF's oddities thwarted her. McCurdy's office rivalled Ebenezer Scrooge's — not a computer in sight. And the old witch wasted no time in indoctrinating her in WOF's labyrinthine, entirely manual, accounting system. Edith felt she would never come up for air again.

Later though her spirits lifted when Louis, the bike courier, showed up. (No doubt he was Ava's lover.) McCurdy obediently released the front door for him using a button in the knee-hole of her desk. The old sourpuss took her lunch break exactly at 12:59 pm, returning to glower at Edith at 1:56 pm. Even better, she left Edith alone for the near-hour, muttering that she needed a break from 'negative energy'.

Next day, at precisely 1:02 pm, Edith disengaged the lock on WOF's front door. She made her way to the park's fountain, slumped down on the bench, and set out the battered paper coffee cup that she'd hidden in her underwear. Easy to summon up some tears. All she had to do was remember what Paul had done to her. Water streamed from her eyes and nose and brought coins like magic.

Her forays into the park quickly became a habit. A tiny trickle of cash, but prison had taught her patience. To escape, she needed money. WOF's skimpy petty cash, afloat in a battered chocolate box on the sea of papers covering McCurdy's desk, would serve as a sweetener for her last day.

Soon the lure of the internet café across the park overcame her. She took her precious coins, skirted her usual bench by the fountain, entered the café and paid for a password. Her hands trembled as they hovered over the sticky keyboard.

She entered Paul's name into the search engine. They'd caught her doing that in the prison library. She'd lost her computer privileges – something about a restraining order. Well, no one could stop her now.

The Shipmaster Financial website flared up on the screen. There he was, as beautiful as the day she'd first seen him, too perfect to be real. Listed as Vice President of Hedge Funds.

Edith wiped her eyes. That first day he'd flashed his electrifying smile at her. She'd actually turned around, thinking he meant someone behind her. He couldn't possibly have noticed her in Shipmaster's vast cube farm.

But he had.

Whenever he passed her in the elevator or in the hall, he'd throw her that smile, or in boring staff meetings, a wink. A lush secret pact between them.

One day, her boss, Miguel Rio, made her Paul's personal assistant. She couldn't believe it. This piercing, perfect feeling must be joy, she thought. Working with Paul left her breathless. If his hand chanced to brush against hers, strange contractions slammed into her abdomen. At first the sensations horrified her, but later she craved them. They would come when Paul had his shirt collar open, or when he put a rose on her desk. They were most intense at night when she huddled in bed alone in her tiny apartment.

For once in her life, she felt special. Perhaps she wasn't a scrawny dull nerd after all. Maybe she did possess a subtle beauty that only Paul could see. She coloured her hair, bought new clothes, tossed out her hoard of romance novels. And then she learned that they shared something more exciting than mere sex.

Edith glanced at the café's clock. Well past two. She was seriously late.

When she scurried into McCurdy's office, the old vulture pounced at once. Mrs. Flood wished to speak with her. Edith felt ill.

Ava's enamelled pink lipstick matched the rose in the lapel of her smart black suit. "McCurdy is missing $2.50 from petty cash," she announced without preamble. "And Louis spotted you in the internet café today."

"You should be worried about every nickel," Edith shot back. "Judging by your financial statements, your precious WOF is sinking like the Titanic." Once a thief, always a thief, she thought. After she shop-lifted that sparkly brooch in high school, the teachers fingered her for every little thing that went missing.

"I am still waiting for your explanation." Ava tap-tapped her pen on her desk.

"OK, McCurdy's too senile to count properly."

"Leaving you alone with the petty cash was a test. A test you have failed."

"If I wanted the petty cash, I'd take all of it. Why don't you check McCurdy's pockets?"

"How dare you! McCurdy is a person of utmost integrity."

"Sure, and she hates me."

"Ridiculous! After everything she has suffered."

"And I haven't?"

"You have no idea what it means to lose a child."

"At least she had a child."

"Enough!" Ava caught her lower lip with her sharp, bleached white teeth. "You will go to your room. I will decide what to do with you after dinner."

You know where you can put your horrid meals, Edith thought as she charged down the staircase past St. Michael's window into McCurdy's office. No McCurdy. She heard the flush of a toilet from the adjoining bathroom. A simple matter to snatch the chocolate box, disengage the front door lock and charge into the park. She slumped down on her usual bench.

Larceny – that's what she and Paul shared in their hearts. At their lunch at his men's club — a place with white table cloths, heavy silverware and classical art on the walls — he'd shared his suspicions about their boss, Miguel. The old shark was skimming millions, he told her. What if they diverted a trickle of that illicit stream into their own off-shore account? Miguel wouldn't dare inform the police because he'd expose his own fraud.

Edith had hesitated, knowing it was wrong. Paul confided how his ex-wife had bankrupted him. He longed to escape with Edith to make a new life. But they needed the money.

That night Paul came to her apartment. So many times she had conjured him up in the late hours, imagining him beside her. When he made love to her, she understood why the French called sex *la petite morte*. Her body was on fire. She'd dare anything for their future.

Paul was brilliant and creative, everything she was not. He assured her that he'd guide her every step of the way. She was clever at hacking into secure sites – he'd spotted her mischief-making on Shipmaster's computer long ago – so using the laptop in her apartment, they embarked on their adventure. She didn't always follow the leaps in his logic, but funds flowed like magic into their account. So much money. Finally she begged him to stop. They had enough.

The sun was setting. A chill darkness crept over her bench, the way it had in that hotel room where she'd sat waiting for Paul, her suitcase on her knees. When the knock came on the door, it wasn't her lover, but the police.

No one believed her when she revealed that she and Paul were a couple. On the contrary, they accused her and Miguel of being an item. Especially after Paul testified that he'd seen them together. And Miguel's user ID was linked to the stream of money diverted to Edith's off-shore account. Unfortunately Miguel couldn't confirm or deny anything because he'd been shot dead. Murdered. In a hotel room two doors away from Edith's.

Edith's lawyer advised her to confess to killing Miguel. To return the money that had mysteriously vanished from her off-shore account. But no one wanted to listen when she tried to tell the truth. It was just like school when she complained to the teachers about the bullies. Ugly and unpopular, no one believed her then. No one believed her now.

In the end, they'd dropped the murder charges against her for lack of physical evidence. She admitted though to the computer fraud. After all, she was guilty of that. And guilty of enormous stupidity. For believing a handsome man would find her attractive. Paul had played her like a violin. All her life people had told her that she was nothing, and they were right.

She pried open the lid to the chocolate box. Empty. So McCurdy had out-foxed her again. Freezing and hungry, she retreated back to WOF. Robin met her in the lobby after the lock on the revolving door clunked open to let her in.

"Oh, Edith, why did you run away?" The young woman couldn't stop fidgeting. "Ava is so angry. They're meeting about you upstairs."

"Here." Edith tossed her the chocolate box. She stormed across the dark, silent lobby. The colour had gone out of St. Michael's window. Too bad. She'd enjoyed imagining Ava Flood as the demon cringing under the hooves of the saint's horse.

On the second floor, McCurdy's querulous voice leaked past the partially open door to Ava's office. "Out of control…"

"Agreed." Ava sounded resigned. "WOF is a rose garden…protect…"

Edith strained her ears, ignoring Robin creeping up behind her.

Louis's flippant voice said, "Your solution's kind of risky, ladies."

Edith's fist tightened on the banister. What did he mean?

And then Ava said, "No choice...remove weeds...her or WOF."

For a heart beat, Edith's strength fled her body. Recovering, she raced upstairs to her room. She jammed a chair under the handle of her door. With trembling hands, she retrieved her precious money from its hiding place in one of Ava's tomes, hollowed-out prison style. Fighting to control her breathing, she foraged under her bed for her back-pack.

Robin's light footsteps approached. A tentative knock. "Edith, please let me in."

Not in a million years.

She stood up, hefting her pack. The coins gave it satisfying weight. She might have a fighting chance, if she took them down one at a time, like that little mouse, Robin.

She tore open the door.

Robin threw up her hands. "Edith, don't!"

"You sent me here. Now they're going to kill me."

"I'm your friend."

Sensing a trap, Edith backed away.

"They're still talking," Robin went on. "I've put something in McCurdy's chocolate box to help you. See for yourself."

"Why should I trust you?"

"I-I'm the one who sent you those letters. I never believed you had anything to do with Miguel Rio's murder."

Edith hesitated a moment. "Don't follow me." She turned and dove down the stairs. Thankfully, Ava was still meeting with her minions, their voices sibilant whispers.

Heart pounding, Edith stole down to the ground floor. She grabbed the chocolate box from McCurdy's desk.

Clutching it to her thin chest, she crouched down, fumbling for the release button. In the still night air, Ava and the others wouldn't fail to hear the lock release. Her eyes bored a straight path to the front door.

She pushed the button.

She heard their shouts before she scrambled back to her feet. She sprinted for the revolving door, her outstretched hand pounding the glass as they stormed down the stairs. She stumbled on WOF's stone steps. Gasping, she hauled herself up and ran.

And kept on running.

At the corner stood a bus, its windows islands of light in a sea of darkness. She thumped its metal side, wheezing for air. Miraculously, its doors flew open.

She threw a handful of coins into the fare box. With a shrug, the driver closed the doors. She collapsed on the bench behind him. Through the large rear window, she spotted Ava and McCurdy, black shadows in the light streaming through WOF's front door. And Louis, leaping onto his bike to give chase.

No other passengers on the bus. The driver turned through twisting streets, gliding past deserted stops, hesitating at stop signs. Louis's fast-pedaling form melted into the darkness behind them.

Edith pressed her fingers to her dry lips. Louis would drag her off the bus. Would the driver help her? She met his skeptical gaze in the rear view mirror. Not a chance. On her own as usual.

The driver braked abruptly, nearly tumbling her to the rubber floor. She spotted a brilliant white sign bearing Toronto Transit's logo. The subway!

With a cry, she leapt to the rear exit door. Pounded on its glass window. The door jerked open, flipping her onto the curb. Pain screamed from her scraped hands. She staggered up, grabbing her pack by its straps, and plunged into the cold white light flowing up the subway stairs.

She landed in the ticket area. No time to fumble for money. She climbed over the waist-high metal barrier, blocking out the shouts of the ticket seller. She was over and down the closest set of stairs before the woman could crack open the door to her booth.

Edith pounded through the connecting tunnel and crept up the steps to the southbound platform. The instant she emerged Louis cried out from where he stood on the northbound side. He was through the turnstile and heading for the connecting passage-way in an instant.

A faint breath rustled her hair. A sigh in the tunnel. A train at last.

She dashed to the end of the platform as it pulled in. Away from the stairway and Louis. He appeared now, running without hesitation. Why, why wouldn't the doors to the train open? They slid open with infinite slowness. She threw herself into the carriage. Looked up and saw Louis bounding through the door at the front. She stared, fighting for breath as he approached, senses alert for the warning chime.

One second after the chimes ceased she threw herself at the doors. She barreled through the gap, the rubber-edged doors nearly crushing her ribs as she wriggled through. Her pack tore as she jerked it free. Louis hit the doors but they held firm. As he was borne away by the train, she threw him the finger.

She quickly left the station, avoiding the irate ticket seller. She set off on foot, sticking to the shadows, heading for the office towers that glittered in the distance. Once she had feared the dark. Now it enveloped her like a friend.

Dawn found her shivering on a damp bench by the harbor. She gulped down breakfast in a doughnut shop with only the homeless for company. Might as well get used to it. She'd be one of them soon. But there was something she had to do first.

At 8:25 am – not 8:24 or 8:26 – she entered the marble lobby of Shipmaster Financial's gold-plated office tower. How familiar it was even after five years. Her feet moved of their own accord to the elevators.

What if the security guard spotted her shabby clothes and backpack? Threw her out? What if she ran into one of her former co-workers? Nothing scared finance people more than poverty. But no one paid her the slightest attention. Maybe people were right – middle-aged women were invisible.

So much the better.

She rode up in an empty elevator. On the 35th floor she got off, made her way to the fire stairs, pried open the door and stepped onto the landing. Safely alone, she dumped out her pack. The chocolate box crashed to the floor.

She stared at a handle bound in black tape. At a knife blade honed to an evil dart. Robin's gift — a prison shiv.

How had timid little Robin got hold of *that?* What the hell was she thinking giving it to her?

Footsteps in the corridor. Edith shoved the knife into her pocket. She grabbed the cleaning fluid and rubber gloves she'd 'borrowed' from WOF's bathroom, pulled a greying T-shirt over her jeans, and jammed everything else back into the pack.

Shipmaster's lobby art now featured uplifting messages superimposed on serene landscapes. Even spirituality pushes product these days, Edith observed sourly. The receptionist didn't throw her a second glance. After all, cleaners didn't qualify as life forms.

She glided through Shipmaster's cube farm invisible to the workers transfixed by their flat-screened monitors. Roaming through the quiet suite of executive offices, she found the one signed Hedge Funds. The corner office. The one with the view of the lake. The one Paul had craved.

She gripped the brass handle with her gloved hand. Not locked. The door swung open.

Paul was talking on a tiny, gold-plated cell phone, his back to her, framed by the vista of office towers and the choppy blue waters of the lake. Only an icy glass sculpture and a photo of his Porsche adorned his ultra-modern black desk.

"The rack of lamb was sub-standard," he was saying. "I'm down to the short strokes on this deal. You fire that chef and get someone competent..." He jumped at the sound of his door closing. He spun around, clicking his phone shut. "Who the hell are you?"

"Paul..." Now that she had her moment, the moment she'd planned for five years, words died in the dust of her throat. "Paul..."

"Edith?" Paul's fine brows shot up. "How did you get in?" He leaned forward, one hand outstretched.

"Don't call security."

"Who's going to stop me? You? What the hell—"

The shiv leapt into her hand. Her heart was pounding, but the blade didn't waver. "Sit down. Don't touch anything."

"OK, OK, take it easy." He dropped into the leather chair behind his desk, highly amused. "Say what you have to say, but short sound bites, OK? I have a client meeting."

"You used me."

"So easy, right? Admit it, you're not the brightest bulb on the Christmas tree."

"Shut up!" She brandished the knife, one hand braced on the desk. "Answer me or forget your client meeting. Forever."

"Fine, ask away." He leaned back, polished, smug even. Five years had blurred and twisted his features somehow. Why had she found him beautiful?

"Miguel Rio wasn't skimming the money from Shipmaster. You were. You used Miguel's user ID to cover your tracks. But you ran across another hacker in Shipmaster's computer system – me! Only a matter of time till I discovered your games. You neutralized me to keep the money."

"Guess you had time in jail to think for once."

"How could you, Paul? I loved you."

"Oh, for God's sake."

Edith saw him glance at his watch in blatant boredom. She wiped her eyes with her free hand. "Miguel was onto you, wasn't he?"

"Yeah, one day he actually did some work after his three-martini lunch."

Breathing grew hard. "You killed him, didn't you?"

"Bull shit."

"Don't lie to me!" She flashed the knife. At last she detected a glimmer of fear in those astonishing blue eyes.

"Grow up, Edith. It was him or me or lose $50 million. Be glad you just went to jail."

"Murderer! Give me the passwords to your off-shore accounts."

"Just like that?"

"You have to pay back the money. Clear Miguel's name. And you owe me, too, you bastard!"

"You stupid bitch!" He had the glass sculpture. Raised above his head. Crashing down.

Edith could never sort out what happened next. Perhaps those scuffles in prison had quickened her defences. Suddenly millions of pieces of glass were everywhere. Paul was leaping over the desk like a wild animal. A stranger she'd never imagined.

His weight knocked the wind right out of her. She didn't have the breath to scream at the pain in her wrist, her back, her belly. He wasn't moving. She wriggled out from under, heaving him over.

He sprawled across his fine silk carpet, the shiv punched through his Turnbull and Asser shirt. His eyelids fluttered. A convulsion shivered through his body.

"Oh, Paul..."

She checked the pulse in his throat. Dead! As dead as her kitten when her father ran over it.

"Oh, Paul, I didn't mean to..."

She waited in silence. Waited for the security guards to burst through the door. But no one came.

She sat up. What if Paul really had lined his office walls with lead to prevent corporate spying? He'd promised he'd do it if he became Vice President. What if no one had heard the commotion?

The shiv came away with some effort. Strangely, only a little blood leaked out. Hands shaking, she gathered up her cleaning lady props and wrapped the horrid blade in a rag.

One last thing. She snatched the silver-framed photo from the desk, tore out the print of Paul's gleaming black Porsche and checked the back. Still a creature of habit. She shoved the photo into her jeans.

No one in sight. Not believing her luck, she eased out of Paul's office. In a heartbeat she was back on the fire stairs.

She couldn't stop shaking while she stripped off the rubber gloves and changed back into her usual clothes. She dropped the shiv back into the chocolate box, picked up her pack and ran.

Each cement step shook a hard vibration up her body as she charged down the fire stairs. Her legs felt flabby and useless. The floor numbers flashed by in a blur. She burst through the emergency door at the bottom and collapsed sobbing on the stained concrete of the alley.

I killed Paul.

She heard the sirens now. Police cars, ambulances and fire trucks poured into the street in front of the office tower.

They'll never believe it was self-defense. No one ever believes me.

Hitching the pack on her shoulder, she headed into a tangle of side streets, letting the noises fade behind her.

Think, brain, think.

She passed tattoo parlors, cheap food places, sex shops and steam baths. She crept into a deserted alley. Kneeling next to a sewer grate, she dropped the chocolate box and the wicked silver shiv through the iron bars, hearing a splash far below her.

Finished, she shuffled back through the seedy streets.

Now what? They'll put me away for life.

A young man was leaning on his bike outside a Chinese noodle bar. It couldn't be! Edith started, galvanized out of her misery. Louis, the bike courier, looked up. Recognized her at once.

"Edith, wait!"

She plunged into the lane behind her, running madly. She crashed into a pungent dumpster. Hard, raucous music throbbed out of the bar that gave onto the alley. In the furtive darkness, the spangling of a costume. A stripper came out the back entrance and lit a cigarette. She saw Edith and smiled.

Louis's bike skidded to a stop in front of her.

"Go away!" Edith shouted.

"Stop running, for heaven's sake. Ava wants to help you."

"Like Hell. You see this?" She jabbed a finger. "This is the face of a killer."

"What? What are you talking about?"

"Is he bothering you?" the stripper broke in.

"Yes!" Edith tore up the stairs, sheltering beside that sparkling costume. The woman held open the door to the bar. Edith stumbled through moist darkness and the sweet stench of beer. She crashed out the other side of the tavern into the sunshine. Louis didn't follow.

No one cares about bag ladies. Must get to a homeless shelter. They'll never find me there.

She wandered through alley after alley, street after street until the day's light began to ebb. She couldn't find the homeless shelters and dared not ask for directions. Any sudden noise or movement made her jump. She imagined police lying in wait around every corner.

The stores began to look familiar. Somehow her random wanderings had led her back to the park across from WOF.

Life's little ironies.

She found her usual bench by the fountain. What did she feel? What did a killer feel? Sadness, yes. Guilt, definitely. But also a strange lightness, a release almost. Face it – she was fated to kill Paul, destined to spend the rest of her life in jail.

She got to her feet. *I'm ready for the police now.*

Oddly enough, WOF's revolving door let her in. The setting sun glowed through the stained glass window of St. Michael, who, she decided, was really far more beautiful than Paul.

Now what?

A long narrow table stretched across the lobby. On it stood a silver champagne bucket, glistening with moisture. She saw dozens of pink roses everywhere. And four people drinking out of sparkling crystal glasses.

A celebration? Nothing about WOF surprised her any more.

"Hey, you made it," Louis said, glass in hand.

Robin rushed over and hugged her. "Oh, Edith, thank heavens you came back."

Edith shook her off. "I killed Paul."

"We know," Ava replied, taking a sip of champagne. She had on a tailored white dress embroidered with pink roses.

"Here," McCurdy said gruffly and shoved a brimming glass into Edith's hand.

"You're all mad," Edith shouted. "Call the police!"

"Not in a million years." Ava flashed her a brilliant smile. "You see, Miguel Rio was my husband."

"But-but you don't have the same name!"

"Mom uses the business name 'Flood'," Louis explained. "'Rio' means river in Spanish. Close enough."

The pack slipped from Edith's fingers. "So that's why you wanted me for your Miracles pilot. That's why McCurdy and Robin never left me alone."

"Of course," Ava said. "Robin told us you were obsessed with Paul. I prayed you'd lead us to something – anything — to clear Miguel's name."

"Mom's broke. She's spent all her money on lawyers and private detectives," Louis said.

"Never mind that WOF is nearly bankrupt. When I heard the news, that Paul had been murdered by an unknown assailant, why, I felt reborn!" Ava declared. "At last my poor Miguel has had justice."

"I've always said you should adopt a hard line when healing victims of social crimes," McCurdy said.

"You're right. It's time to rethink my philosophy," Ava replied, reaching for a fresh champagne bottle.

"And to deal with that drunk driver who killed my son," McCurdy went on.

"I know, you've waited far too long," Ava replied, resting her hand on the older woman's shoulder.

No wonder they all liked St. Michael, Edith thought. He's the avenging angel. "But I didn't mean to kill Paul," she confessed. "Robin should never have given me that knife."

"I used it on that animal who raped me at the half-way house," the young woman shot back. "He'll never harm another woman now. And Paul would have killed you the same way he killed Miguel."

Edith stared into her drink, knowing she was right.

"Before you arrived, we were discussing whether you should join our special little family," Ava said. "Robin insists, but I fear that you are rather a wild card. You take bold risks. Perhaps too bold."

"She gets things done," Louis put in.

"And WOF must automate to survive," McCurdy said. "We need her computer expertise."

Light flamed down from St. Michael's silver sword and shot through Edith's sparkling champagne. "I think," she said slowly, pulling Paul's photo with his passwords from her jeans, "that I may have the solution to your financial problems right here. As part of my rehabilitation, I'll recover Shipmaster Financial's millions. WOF can return it discreetly, no questions asked — for a percentage, of course."

"In that case, what can I say?" Ava beamed. "We shall have to adjust to one another."

Edith polished off her champagne and held out her glass for a refill. "And since we're talking business, I've thought of a much better name for WOF."

They all looked at her expectantly.

"The Widows and Orphans Fund."

CHRISTMAS IN ALICE

Our visit to Alice Springs in Australia led to this story. Although the resort hotel is fictional, the Henley Boat Races on Old Todd are indeed real.

Published in Blood on the Holly, A Christmas Anthology, *Caro Soles ed., Baskerville Books, 2007.*

From the moment she sent her reply to Eileen's email, Margaret fretted that she'd made a mistake. She brought up the subject over breakfast, interrupting Brian's sacrosanct morning ritual, his hunt through the pages of the *Sydney Morning Herald* for the latest sin committed by Australia's prime minister.

"Eileen Grady?" he asked, the reading glasses slipping down his nose as he lowered the paper. "You mean your peculiar friend from graduate school in Vancouver?"

"For heaven's sake, Brian, that was 30 years ago. People change."

"Not that one."

But we've all changed, Margaret thought. She was no longer the slim cross-country runner Brian had married. She hated the soggy wads of fat around her middle. "Eileen's lived, as we all have," she said. "We have no idea what direction her life has taken. What she's accomplished, what's happened to her." She leaned forward, teasing his paper with her forefinger. "Admit it, you'd love catching up on old scandals in my chemistry lab."

"Spare me." Brian glared at the editorial as though his outrage could restore the moral centre of Oz's political system. "That bloody internet. Just leads to 'googling' ancient friends for fun and profit. How convenient that Eileen's tour dumps her in Sydney."

She watched him turn a page. "Brian, it's not right to leave her on her own for Christmas."

"I was looking forward to being on our own, now that our daughter has buggered off." Brian threw her his naughty boy look. "Enjoying the surf on Bondi Beach with the wife on Christmas Day, that's what I want. I've had enough obligations for a lifetime. As have you."

She launched her final volley. "I've haven't been back to Canada since we were married. Not once. Eileen's my chance to reconnect."

"The past is gone. I never think about it." But he sighed and closed the paper, signaling capitulation. "You're too damn nice, that's your problem."

***

No further emails from Eileen appeared. Margaret assumed that she'd simply call on Christmas Eve summoning them to pick her up. Eileen had never been adept at communication – she acted as though others should sense what she wanted and grew petulant when they didn't respond.

On reflection, this was probably why the other graduate students avoided her. At the time Margaret attributed their attitude to academic snobbery. She and her friends worked for a name professor whose lab sprawled over the top floor of the chemistry building. But close to the stairwell lurked the small dark lab of a minor researcher. She'd often noticed Eileen there sealing up fluids in glass tubes for analysis. She wasn't sure what led her to befriend the pale, sharp-nosed girl. Was it because so few women ventured into chemistry? Perhaps, but she also felt protective of Eileen as though she could entice her out of her social awkwardness and transform her into someone more confident and attractive. Or to be honest, more socially acceptable.

Initially Eileen had been cool to Margaret's efforts at friendship. But one day she surfaced next to Margaret's bench, brown bag lunch in hand. From then on they had lunch together nearly every day.

"She fancies you," Brian had taunted her.

"Don't be ridiculous. You don't like her because she's nerdy."

"Face it, you only hang about that white-coated ninny to showcase your own good looks."

Looks that had pretty much faded now, Margaret thought, catching a glimpse of herself in the hall mirror.

In anticipation of Eileen's visit, she tidied their multi-level house – one of Brian's early designs – and unearthed the Christmas decorations she'd shoved to the back of the storage room because Alison wouldn't be home for the holidays. She was surprised how sad she felt when she uncurled the branches of their artificial tree and popped on the ornaments. No point celebrating Christmas without Alison.

They spent Christmas Eve at home waiting. Brian did his usual 20 lengths in the pool while she read a paperback novel in the shade, admiring the hard muscles she knew hid under the soft layer of his freckled skin. When they still had no word by late afternoon, she cooked their favourite meal of lamb cutlets and garlic mashed potatoes. No Christmas presents, Brian had decided, but he cracked open a bottle of bubbly. Best to start the holidays off with a bang while they still had privacy, he teased her as it grew dark, coaxing her down under the tree, the sparkling ornaments twirling in a breath of wind through the French windows.

She woke to the penetrating cry of the telephone. She sat up in the night, not knowing where she was. Brian mumbled something beside her — they'd fallen asleep under the tree. The phone kept ringing. Alison, she thought, stumbling over the sheepskin rug, fumbling for the receiver.

The voice was unfamiliar, authoritative. "This is Constable Owen of the Alice Springs Police Force. Am I speaking to Mrs. Margaret Dennis?"

The police, oh God, it's Alison. Blood hammered in her ears.

"Do you know an Eileen Grady?" The woman repeated the question with more than a hint of impatience. "She put you down as her contact in Australia. There's been an accident."

***

"You don't have to go," Brian said later at the airport while she checked her boarding pass. Only one seat left on the night flight to Alice Springs this Christmas Eve. "She isn't hurt."

"She's in shock. We can't just leave her," Margaret said.

"Trust Eileen — histrionic to the last."

"That's not fair. The police don't know what happened."

"Yes, and when you're talking to the police, make sure you tell them about Laura."

Margaret stared him. "What possible good would that do?"

"Payback for buggering our Christmas." His resentful face haunted her as she passed through security and boarded the plane.

***

The flight to Alice Springs headed west into the dark. Margaret huddled under the thin airline blanket, wishing she'd brought a sweater. It was always so cold on planes.

Laura. She hadn't thought about that poor girl in years. In that way she was no better than Brian, avoiding unpleasantness by dismissing the past. She stared out the window, imagining Sydney's red tile roofs and turquoise lozenges of swimming pools passing below. The green of the coast would quickly give way to the cracked tan of the desert.

When Alison was five, Brian had hired a Land Rover to drive from Darwin to Adelaide during the holidays. But they hadn't counted on the vast empty distances and the liquid pressure of the heat. Alison grew restless, constantly fighting Margaret's rules about wandering into the wild with its venomous snakes and spiders. Not even a visit to a camel farm with a tame dingo settled her down. And the flies, everywhere the flies. Landing on their food, crawling on their bare arms and faces whenever they left the car, hovering in a hissing black fog over a forlorn kangaroo carcass, a victim of the road trains that hurtled down the highway.

Australia's ancient mountains, once higher than the Himalayas, had dwindled to 1000 foot nubs. All rivers flowed to the deep-set heart of the continent and vanished underground feeding a strange, otherworldly nature — the Garden of Eden designed by Hieronymus Bosch. Flowers sprouted from tree trunks, not the tips of branches. Incongruous black oak trees split in half when their roots struck artesian water. And ghost gum trees reared up like forked white lightning in their headlights nearly forcing them off the road.

Their journey had ended, oddly enough, in Alice Springs.

***

The plane landed in a rain storm. 15 years before, Alice's legendary reservoir had nearly run dry, but now dark drops hammered the windows of the shuttle bus into town.

"Unusual to get rain on Christmas Day," the driver told her. "Hope you're not travelling into the outback. Most roads are flooded out."

Of course, Margaret thought, the parched earth absorbed no more water than a stone. People could drown in the desert.

"Got to take the long way around. Can't use the bridge," he went on. "Todd River is near to setting a record."

Margaret shivered. The police officer found Eileen near that bridge. She remembered the Todd, a dry river bed thick with straw grass and punctured by black oaks. With the rains, water would rage through it, a torrent metres deep

The driver dropped her off at the police station, a low concrete building near the centre of town. In the dusky pre-dawn the waiting room rested in church-like silence. No one there except an elderly woman lying on a bench by the wall and a police officer sitting at the reception desk in a pool of light.

"I'll tell Constable Owen you're here," he said when Margaret told him her name. He stood up, straightening his khaki short-sleeved shirt and shorts.

A soft noise made Margaret take a closer look at the old woman. Her heart raced. It couldn't be. "Eileen?" she ventured.

"Yes, Margaret, it's me." The words came out in a whisper. Margaret knelt down beside her and took her hand. It was icy cold.

The woman's stone grey eyes scanned Margaret's face and figure. "You look the same," she said.

Margaret struggled to return the false compliment. She tried to detect traces of the young Eileen buried under the clay of age.

"I see you've found each other," said a woman's deep voice.

Margaret looked up at an indigenous Australian of Brobdingnagian proportions.

"We spoke on the phone. Might I have a word, Mrs. Dennis?"

***

Constable Owen showed Margaret into an interview room and closed the door. "I need you to get your friend to tell us what happened," she said.

"But you already know." The close air hurt Margaret's throat. "You said she's in shock."

"No, I said she's not talking. That's different. The paramedics with the flying doctor service looked her over. She's OK."

"She's on her own. In a strange place."

"No worries. Oz is a strange place. Full of strange people." Owen smiled, not without irony.

"Eileen doesn't do well in nature," Margaret said. "Something happened back in university."

One weekend she had talked Eileen into coming along on a hike. Most graduate students, even architecture students like Brian, embraced outdoor sports as an antidote to academia. Camping expeditions doubled as parties. But Margaret hadn't understood how excruciating climbing the slopes of Diamond Head Mountain could be for someone unfit. Red-faced and wheezing, Eileen fell half a mile behind the others. Brian had to carry her pack after she sat down on the trail too tired and stubborn to budge. He had to put up her tent, as well. Worse, she'd forgotten to bring food so she had to get by on what Margaret and Brian could spare and on the grudging donations of the others.

"Bad idea to bring her, love. She's an epic disaster," Brian said later when he crawled into Margaret's tent. But the full catastrophe was yet to come.

At midnight they woke to shrill cries of animal terror. People raced out of their tents into the moonless night. In the dark confusion of hurtling bodies, Eileen's tent got knocked over. Only at daybreak did they realize that she had disappeared.

"So where was she?" Owen asked.

"The Mounties – the rescuers – found her in the woods below the campsite. She was pretty banged up. No one knows what happened."

"Really. She didn't tell you?"

"I felt responsible. She was off work for weeks. When she came back to the lab, I never pressed her about it."

"So what do you think happened?"

Margaret swallowed, remembering the heat and the dirt, the flies and mosquitoes. "Well, hiking's tough if you're not used to it. I think she woke up in the dark and panicked."

"But Alice is civilized – at least we locals like to think so. And it's only a short walk from Eileen's hotel to Old Todd."

Margaret had a sudden vivid memory of the indigenous people wandering through the Todd's dry riverbed, so silent and sad they seemed to be walking through another dimension. "Why all the questions?" she asked. "You found her. She's OK."

"Right you are. It's Eileen's friend I'm worried about."

"Isn't she back at the hotel?"

Owen's shrewd dark eyes took her in. "I told you about Mrs. Redding when I called."

Margaret glanced down at her hands. "I-I'm sorry. When you phoned, I thought it was about my daughter, Alison. She and her boyfriend are camping in the Northern Territory this Christmas, you see. Once I realized she was safe, I simply didn't take in much more."

"No worries." Owen checked her note book. "Eileen and Phyllis Redding took a stroll yesterday evening. When they didn't turn up for their group's farewell supper, the tour director called us. Apparently Phyllis said she was keen on photographing the Henley Boat Races on Old Todd. Bit odd. I found Eileen OK but..." She spread a large palm.

"Phyllis is missing."

"Right you are. The two ladies were sharing accommodation to save on the single supplement fee. The tour company set it up." She smiled again. "I'm told it wasn't a love match."

No, roommates don't work out for Eileen, Margaret thought.

"Let's hope my mates find Phyllis wandering about just a bit damp," Owen said. "Hate finding bodies after a flood. Nasty, especially after the dingoes and insects have had a go. You all right, Mrs Dennis?"

"Is-is Eileen under arrest?" Margaret stammered.

Owen snapped her notebook shut. "No, she's free to go. But no buggering off to Canada till I get a statement."

***

Owen drove them to the hotel in her land rover. A cold galaxy of faint blue lights wreathed the resort's entrance way. Margaret recognized it as the place where she, Brian and Alison had stayed 15 years before and said so.

"What brought you to Alice?" Owen asked.

"My daughter got ill – appendicitis. We spent Christmas here after she left hospital," Margaret said.

They entered the lobby. The lively family-run hotel she remembered had been much expanded and renovated, and hardened into a standardized resort. The tacky plastic Santa Claus that had cheered up Alison was long gone, replaced by a spiky white artificial tree.

"Imogen will look after you," Owen said, indicating the blond girl behind the reception desk. "Do your best to have a Merry Christmas." She touched the brim of her straw hat and left them.

Imogen sported a spotless safari suit and a brass name tag. Stepping away from the desk, she explained that she'd put them together in a new room.

"I want *my* room," Eileen said in a loud, clear voice, startling them.

The girl hesitated. "I'm sorry, Constable Owen asked us to secure it until Mrs. Redding's son arrives from Florida. We'll do our best to look after you."

"Imogen won't lift a finger," Eileen said once they were settled. She slumped down on the end of one of the twin beds. "I want my things."

Margaret dropped her overnight bag beside the writing desk. "Do you want me to call anyone?" she asked.

Eileen shook her head.

Margaret watched Eileen kick off her clumsy walking shoes. "It's been a long time," she began, not knowing what else to say. "What have you been doing with yourself?"

"Don't act like you don't know."

"Be fair, Eileen. We lost touch after I moved to Australia." She thought for a moment. "Don't tell me you stayed with the chemistry department?"

Eileen shrugged. Her mouth curved up, a strange, sly smile.

"After everything that happened," Margaret couldn't help saying. "My God, why didn't you move on?"

"Nobody gave me a job off campus. And now..." Her fists twisted the limp fabric of her khaki trousers. "The department let me go. Nobody wants technicians over 50."

"I'm sorry. I didn't know."

"I always wanted to visit Australia." Eileen's slack features bunched up. "The tour company lied to me. All they did was march me through gift stores. They took all my money. And they made me share a room with that stupid plastic woman."

Margaret let out a breath. "Look, you've been through a lot. Why don't we get cleaned up? You shower first. I need to call Brian."

"You're still with him."

"Yes, of course, I am." The years peeled away. She'd forgotten how much Eileen's words could sting. "And we have a daughter, Alison. She's 20."

"Everyone else in your lab got divorced."

"What about you? Do you have family?"

"Don't be ridiculous." Eileen vanished into the bathroom. A heartbeat later, the shower roared to life.

Alone now, Margaret phoned home. She counted the rings, thumbing through the postcards thoughtfully provided by the resort – for a small fee, of course. Images of kangaroos, Aboriginal dot paintings and a strange foot race held in the dry Todd River basin. 30 rings, where was Brian? He wouldn't have gone to the pub. He promised her he wouldn't. The frigid air conditioning made her tremble.

The bathroom door flew open nearly making her drop the phone. Eileen emerged, dressed in a white terry cloth robe belonging to the hotel. She dumped her clothes on the floor and got into bed. When Margaret suggested breakfast, she flopped down on her side, her back a ridge of ice.

Slowly, mechanically, Margaret replaced the receiver and picked up the unruly heap of clothes. She draped them over a chair: a thin navy cardigan, a stained white T-shirt and the shapeless khakis. A small silver object thudded to the carpet. A digital camera.

She bent down and quietly slipped it into her purse. Exhausted, but desperate for fresh air, she let herself out of the room.

Outside the rain had stopped, but even under the dull overcast, the desert heat seared her skin. Enormous ghost gum trees edged the hotel driveway. She followed their chalk-white trunks out to the main road, fragments of their brittle bark crunching under her sandals. Immediately the flies sprang upon her, invading her mouth and nostrils.

Beating them off, she hurried down the main road, the incongruous roar of a river filling her ears. She spotted the bridge over Old Todd a short distance away, just as Constable Owen had said.

A rickety metal barrier prevented her from crossing over, but from where she stood on the road, she had a clear view. A foaming brown torrent sluiced under the bridge. Branches and debris tore past. Black oaks leaned like charred match sticks into the flood. No one could survive a fall into those waters, not even a giant like Constable Owen.

Several police officers were searching along the far bank close to the raging river. She recognized Owen who looked up and waved to her. Margaret half-raised her hand in reply. The flies settled on her again. She turned and walked swiftly back to the hotel.

"Cheer up," Imogen said, when Margaret returned. "Grab some tucker from the breakfast buffet. Christmas present from me to you. Do you good."

Perhaps coffee would help, Margaret thought and thanked her. She joined the crush of guests charging the buffet tables set up in the dining room, but her appetite was gone. She filled two bowls of fruit salad, one for herself, one for Eileen, and found a table.

Alone in the crowd, she pulled the digital camera from her purse and switched it on. An image of Uluru in the rain popped up on the screen, the rock's blood red surface laced with streams of water. She flicked through dozens of photos of gaudily dressed tourists who were hugging koalas, brandishing gift store souvenirs or raiding dinner buffets. A cheerful, heavy-set woman centred in a lot of them. Eileen appeared only once, standing next to the white Christmas tree in the lobby, her narrow face barred with shadow.

The last image was black.

"Fine little camera, that." Imogen had appeared at her table. "Lots of you Americans like it."

Margaret slipped it back into her purse.

"Can I ask you something?" Imogen took the chair opposite her. "Have the police found Phyllis?"

Margaret shook her head.

"It's stupid to hope, I know." The girl's face crumpled. "I should have stopped them. Eileen couldn't possibly have meant the Henley Boat Races. I mean, that's stupid. But Phyllis was so keen. She wanted to see every last thing in her guidebook. She was such a lot of fun, such a nice lady. Everybody liked her."

Everybody liked her. That's what they'd said about Laura, too.

"Her son gave her the trip," Imogen went on. "He's flying in tomorrow. He'll never feel the same about Christmas now, will he?"

***

Back in the room, Eileen was sitting up in bed, hands splayed on the sheets. She snatched the bowl of fruit salad from Margaret and stared into it. "Why do they always put in cantaloupe?" she grumbled.

"Eileen, we need to talk," Margaret said, setting her purse down on the writing desk. "About Phyllis Redding." She watched Eileen chew the pieces of woody melon. "Her son will want to know what happened to his mother."

Eileen lifted a bony shoulder. "Nothing happened to her."

"Don't be like that."

Eileen shoved more salad into her mouth.

"If you say nothing, people will think the worst. No one can blame you for an accident."

"Don't treat me like an idiot." Eileen's bowl tipped over, the dregs of syrup staining the sheet.

"I want to help, but I can't if you continue this way."

"OK, fine." Eileen was getting loud. "We were on the bridge. She walked down into the dark."

"What do you mean?"

"I guess she wanted to take a closer look at the river."

Margaret sat down. "Why didn't you stop her?"

"Why should I? She never listened. All she did was talk. Talk, talk, talk. Everything was always so wonderful, like fucking Disneyland."

For an instant something primal flashed into Eileen's face, the way it had in graduate school when she smashed the glass tubes of her failed experiments into the sink, one after the other.

Rage melted into a craftier look. "Since you like asking questions," she said, "why don't you ask me what happened on Diamond Head Mountain?"

"That was 30 years ago."

"And you're dying to find out."

"No, I'm not," Margaret said. In spite of the air conditioning, her dress felt wet and sticky. "But if you want to tell me, I'll listen."

"I was raped."

"That can't be." Margaret's heart beat like a bird's. The dark suspicion she'd never admitted even to herself now had voice. "We were a dozen students camping together. Everyone was safe."

"Oh, come on. A single woman alone in a tent, why that's begging for it. A dried-up virgin needs a hard shag to set her straight."

"You had a dream. A nasty, vivid dream."

"The cops took me to hospital. That wasn't dreaming."

"Did the doctors examine you?"

Eileen turned her face away.

"You didn't tell them." Margaret pressed her arms over her chest willing her heart to slow down. "Why didn't you say something?"

"I was an ugly nerd. They'd just say I was lucky someone bothered to throw me a fuck." She seized the salad bowl. With shocking violence, she shattered it against the wall next to her bed.

After a time, Margaret stood up. She reached out a hand, not quite daring to touch Eileen's shoulder. "I would have believed you," she said.

Eileen stared at the mess on her bed in rigid silence.

"Let's clean this up," Margaret said, pulling on the bed covers. "You'll cut yourself."

"Aren't you going to ask who raped me?" The sly look was back on Eileen's face.

Margaret swallowed. "All right, who did it?"

"Brian."

"You're lying!" The words exploded from Margaret's throat. "Brian would never do that to a woman. And he was with me the whole night."

"Sure about that? He didn't sneak to the outhouse, not even once?"

"No, not even once." Margaret stumbled back to the writing desk and grabbed her purse. "Why did you come to Australia? Why did you look me up? You hated the tour. And you obviously hate Brian and me. I don't understand you. I don't think I ever did."

Unable to look at Eileen, she bolted from the room.

***

Imogen loaned Margaret her office. Closing the door, Margaret dialed home. This time, Brian answered.

"Oh, it's you," he said.

In his voice, she detected the lingering blur of alcohol. "Are you all right?" she asked.

"Of course, I am."

"You were right, I shouldn't have come. I'm leaving Alice. We'll have a proper Christmas."

"Forget Christmas. By the way, your daughter called."

"Alison." Some of the tenseness left her body. "Thank heavens. How is she?"

"That gormless boyfriend dumped her. She was all teary and sentimental about Christmas. She wanted to come home."

"And you told her to come at once. To have a family Christmas with us. You did tell her that, didn't you, Brian? Brian?"

After a pause, he said, "No, I didn't. Christmas is over, and you're not here. What would be the point?"

"Point? She's our only child." Tears burned her eyes. "I want my daughter."

"For God's sake, I can't deal with you crying."

"Did you tell her that I'm here in Alice?"

"Yes, yes, I told her. She'll be fine. Just come home."

"I need to ask you something." She gripped the receiver so tightly she thought it would crack. "Eileen said a strange thing."

"Predictable. All right, out with it."

"You remember our camping trip on Diamond Head Mountain? She said someone attacked her."

"He probably thought her tent was the outhouse."

"That isn't funny! She claims she was *raped*." When Brian didn't reply, she pressed on, desperate to fill the silence. "It would explain why she screamed so horribly. Why she ran off into the woods. Why she wouldn't talk about it after. But she must have got it wrong. Please tell me that she's off her head."

"I don't know," Brian said finally. "I heard the lads talking. Later, a long time after."

"What did they – what did they say?"

"They were having a laugh. Something about chasing a pig through the woods."

"So it's true!" She remembered laughing at the crude humor of Brian's friends, refusing to take it seriously. "You knew. You knew and you did nothing. You should have told the police."

"They were my mates! What would you have me do? Ruin their lives? And you know Eileen's a bloody liar. In the end no one got hurt."

"Now who's the liar?"

"Margaret, for God's sake —"

She slammed down the receiver, smothering his voice. She stared down at the desk feeling that she'd fallen into a vacuum where she could hear and see nothing.

After a time, her eyes focused on a framed photo. It showed Imogen and her friends in an absurd boat, holding it at waist height, their legs poking through its empty bottom. They weren't rowing, they were running like a large, pale-legged insect across the dry Todd river bottom. Printed across the top of the photo, she read, 'The Henley Boat Races'.

No wonder Imogen hadn't believed what she'd overheard Eileen say. Margaret stood up, left the office and headed back outside.

By now the overcast had burned off. The sun was white hot in a sky of hard ceramic blue. She felt its mad carcinogenic rays beating against her bare skin. Her underarms flooded with sweat. Fighting back the flies, she fought her way into town.

By the time she arrived at the police station, she was so dizzy she could barely stand. White spots danced in her vision. A policeman summoned Constable Owen who brought her a plastic bottle of cool water, ordering her to drink it down.

"You're this close to heat stroke, Mrs. Dennis," Owen said, pressing her thick thumb and forefinger together. "You need four litres a day in Alice. Me, I need twice that."

Margaret couldn't laugh. "I have to tell you something," she whispered.

Owen settled her in the same interview room where they'd been earlier that morning. "All right, I'm listening."

"Eileen had a room mate back in university," Margaret began. "Laura was so nice. Everybody liked her." How trite to be echoing Imogen's words about Phyllis Redding, she thought. "Laura worked as a secretary for the chemistry department. She was a very pretty girl. The male students paid her a lot of attention. They didn't find her threatening, the way they did us female grad students."

"Foolish lot men are," Owen grinned. "Laura and Eileen sound like a strange couple."

"Everyone thought that. Laura took Eileen in after that, well, trouble on Diamond Head Mountain. They did everything together, movies, pubs, shopping. Laura even persuaded Eileen to join the university's hiking club. Got her out into nature again. But then Laura found a boyfriend."

"I'll bet that threw a toad into the pudding."

Margaret rubbed her forehead. "They stopped chumming around. Everyone in the department noticed and made mean jokes about it. Especially after Laura asked Eileen to move out. That weekend the hiking club scheduled a walk up the coast. In spite of everything, Eileen insisted on coming along. Somehow she and Laura got separated from the others and took a short-cut over the reservoir. The footpath over the dam is very narrow with a railing on one side. And a 50 foot drop on the other."

Owen opened her notebook.

Margaret closed her eyes. "Eileen said that they were halfway across the dam when Laura lost her balance. The waterfall and the current are so strong it took the searchers six weeks to find her body."

"And you see a pattern."

"I don't know. The coroner and the police said it was an accident, but Laura's parents never accepted it. They hounded Eileen for years. Ruined her life." Margaret wiped her cheeks. "I understand them now. Laura was their only child. I've always believed Eileen, defended her, but after

Phyllis Redding, I, well, I don't know what to think any more."

"Right." Owen closed her notebook. "Thanks for coming in."

"You don't believe me."

"No, I didn't say that. But you just told me that the Canadian authorities decided Laura had an accident."

"Just like Phyllis Redding."

Owen spread her hands. "We're still looking for evidence, Mrs. Dennis."

"I found this in Eileen's pant pocket." Margaret set the silver camera down between them on the table. "It's not hers."

"No worries. I'll ask Phyllis Redding's son about it when he comes in." Owen pulled an evidence bag from the voluminous back pocket of her shorts and sealed the camera inside. "Find any interesting photos?"

"The last picture is black. No light." Margaret licked her lips. "I don't think Phyllis took it."

"I see." Owen studied her for a moment. "Look here, Mrs. Dennis. Why don't you ask Imogen for your own room back at the hotel? And catch the first flight home to Sydney."

***

Imogen was happy to rent her a room far removed from Eileen's. Dead tired, Margaret sank down on her bed, rubbing her sun-burned arms. No point rushing back to Sydney. She couldn't face Brian. Not yet. She needed time to think. About him and their marriage. For she hadn't told Owen that he was Laura's lover.

30 years ago, open relationships were the rage. You weren't supposed to be jealous. At least *women* weren't supposed to be jealous. And Brian's pubs and women had continued for much of their married life, only easing off

when he took early retirement. She'd determinedly ignored that aspect of him to preserve the precious illusion of their family life. But now all she could hear was the silent din of her carefully constructed myth collapsing around her.

Alison, she thought. *All I have left is Alison. Perhaps she's on her way to find me here in Alice. I can always hope.* She looked around for her suitcase and realized that she'd left it behind in Eileen's room.

Her old key still worked. When she swung open the door, she started. Eileen stood in the centre of the room wringing out her white t-shirt, wearing only a bra and the khaki trousers.

"You took something that belongs to me," Eileen said. "I want my camera."

"Stop it," Margaret said, pushing her way in. She spotted her bag next to the writing desk just inside. "We both know that camera isn't yours."

A flash of white. The t-shirt flared out and smacked her wetly on the cheek. "You hit me!"

The wet shirt flew at her again. She seized it and pulled, wrenching Eileen off balance. She seized Eileen's wiry wrists. Pushed with all she had. Eileen crashed onto the bed.

And with surprising agility, sprang back up.

"Stay where you are," Margaret panted. "I know why you came to Australia."

Eileen's hard grey eyes narrowed.

"You've always fancied Brian. That's why you acted so helpless on Diamond Head, getting him to carry your things and to put up your tent. You were hoping he'd crawl into your tent instead of mine, and when he didn't, you staged a scene. But your drama backfired because of his poisonous mates."

"Fuck you."

"Then he took up with Laura. How you must have hated her. And now, when you're at loose ends after getting fired, you travel to Australia, hoping we're divorced. You're pathetic. And Brian's not worth it."

Eileen leapt, knocking her into the writing desk. Her purplish hands grasped the wet shirt like a rope. Margaret tried to fend her off, but Eileen was too strong. An instant later, she felt a crushing force across her throat. Her cry for help became a croak.

She scrabbled madly for Eileen's hair. Scraped her nails over bare flesh. A shriek of outraged pain. She smashed her knee into Eileen's soft belly.

Air rasped back into her lungs. Eileen sprawled on the carpet, legs splayed. Margaret seized her suitcase, clasping it to her chest like a shield. Eileen rolled onto all fours, still holding the wet shirt.

"Don't try it," Margaret coughed. "I'm stronger than you. I always was."

A rap on the door. Enough to distract Eileen for a moment. Margaret scrabbled for the door handle and staggered out into the hall.

A bewildered elderly couple stared at her, saying that they'd heard loud voices. Margaret managed to shake her head. She turned and fled to the safety of her room.

She threw the bolt lock, leaning against her door until her breathing slowed. She must call Constable Owen, tell her what happened. But would Owen believe her? She hadn't believed her about Laura. In fact, she'd told her to bugger off back to Sydney like a good girl.

I'll wait, she thought. *Get clean, and decide what to do.*

She stripped off her rancid clothes and stepped under the shower. She scrubbed herself madly to tear away every speck of the horrid Christmas Day. Still wrapped in the bath towel, she stretched out on the bed, too tired to dress.

The telephone on the bedside table shrilled. What if it was Brian?

Or Eileen?

She let it ring. Finally it stopped.

I can't just lie here, she thought after a time. She dried off, dressed in the shorts and shirt she'd brought and tossed the rest of her belongings into her bag. A sudden bang on the door made her jump with fear.

She crept over to it in her bare feet and peered through the spy hole. Recognized Imogen in her safari suit. She undid the lock and let her in.

"Heavens, you scared me," Imogen said. "I was leaving you a note. Your daughter's here. She's looking for you. I phoned your room, but you didn't answer."

"Alison! Where is she?"

"I saw your friend in the lobby. She said you'd gone for a walk. They went out looking for you."

"When?" Margaret seized the girl's shoulders. "When did they leave?"

"Not five minutes ago. Mrs. Dennis, please, you're hurting me."

"Call the police!"

Margaret tore down the hall. An intense pain crushed her chest, squeezing her heart. Her lungs had no air.

She reached the lobby. Ran out and down the driveway, oblivious to the bursts of pain in her bare feet. Down the road to the bridge. Saw no one. She bent over, sides heaving.

On the far bank, a flicker of movement. She shouted Alison's name, but who would hear her over the roar of the water? Summoning the agility she'd once had as a runner, she leapt over the metal barrier. Caught her foot and fell heavily.

Her face and hands throbbed with pain. Blood flowed from her knee. She staggered up and hobbled across the bridge. *Oh, please, God, let there be two people,* she prayed. *Let there be two.* She rolled over the second barrier and screamed in agony as her knee struck the pavement.

In the dim twilight, she spotted two figures by the river's edge. A tall slender girl with auburn hair and a shorter figure wearing khaki pants.

"Alison," she cried in pure terror.

The rushing river drowned out her voice. She saw Eileen bend down and pick up a large stone.

"Alison!" She screamed with all her passion as a mother.

Instinct made Alison turn at that moment. The blow from Eileen's rock missed her head, but struck her shoulder, knocking her down. Young and agile, she rolled away from the water. Eileen seized the girl's shirt.

Margaret leapt down into the dark. The world slowed. She did not hear the roar of Old Todd or the shouts of Constable Owen and Imogen behind her. She saw only Alison's pale terrified face and the murky torrent boiling past as she tore her child free of those murderous claws.

And hurled Eileen into the river.

INCOMPETENCE KILLS

Ever get fed up with people who really don't know how to do their jobs? That's what led to this flash fiction story.

Published in EFD1: Starship Goodwords, *Donna Carrick ed., Carrick Publishing, 2012.*

Competence is a commodity in low supply. Amazing that the world functions at all really. But incompetence does have an upside: it creates such tempting opportunities for predators.

Like me.

You'd never give me a second glance. In appearance, I'm pale and bland. The only remarkable thing about me is a black spot under my thumbnail. If you bothered to get to know me better, you'd recognize it as a sign of my true nature.

Inconspicuous and invidious.

How trusting you people are. The coffee cup unattended in the food court, the step too close to the subway platform.

Innocent and inattentive.

Lucky for you that I've learned to, shall we say, engineer my violent tendencies.

Take Miranda, for instance, chattering on her phone all day long in the cubicle next to mine. Hardly a conversation, I call it "monversation": a non-stop stream of complaints about her miserable lack of challenge at work. Well, perhaps if she actually did some work for a change.

Indolent and incompetent.

So this morning I gave her the challenge she so fervently desired. I hacked into her computer system and slid a dollop of company cash into her personal bank account. The amount? Perfectly equal to her frightening lawyer's fees, a figure helpfully supplied through the echo-chamber of her office.

Indiscreet and incompetent.

Shock and awe as security marches her off the premises. I rub my black spot, savouring the blissful quiet now that she's gone. And, I want you to take note, no violence necessary.

I soldier on, in blind service to the company, the brave widow in tech support. You see, I'm mourning my dear, departed Barry, once the head of software engineering. Our marriage lasted only a year, how sad. Especially after the hard work to pry him loose from Miranda.

I rub my black spot.

Barry and Miranda, two dullards joined together in a live-in arrangement of convenience. Yes, Barry's paid-off house and his investment portfolio, plumped up by thrift and a boring life, proved convenient indeed.

For me.

Boring and bland on the outside, red fire on the inside. Barry and I were more alike than he ever knew. Quite the challenge to crack his security codes so I could ferret out his favorite kinky websites and become his fantasy woman.

Even if I had to hold my nose to do it.

Intemperate and invidious.

And so we were married. Such a shame Barry insisted on clinging to his old tight-fisted ways. He just didn't believe in the joint ownership of *anything*. Alas, he'd had his own way for far too long, first as an only child indulged by his parents, then pampered for years by Miranda, that doormat.

Intransigent and imprudent.

Barry brought it on himself. You do see that, don't you? I really do try to avoid violence whenever possible. To be honest, I do find it thrilling, but the risk...

Did I mention that I graduated as a biomedical engineer? During one of our more exotic evenings, where I played nurse and Barry became the naughty patient, I injected him with a full vial of insulin, not saline solution as he supposed.

Inconspicuous and inevitable.

My cell phone rings, startling me. Barry's lawyer must see me without delay. I feel an unfamiliar flutter of panic. Barry's will was straightforward, I assure myself. All goes to me. I made sure of that.

But when I arrive at the lawyer's office, she looks distressed. She sits me down.

Turns out Barry stayed as true to his nature as I have to mine. Ten years ago, to protect his money from Miranda, he made her sign a co-habitation agreement. Miranda, that sly bitch, is suing for her share of the spoils.

Impossible and inconceivable.

How could I slip up? I scrutinized every document Barry kept in the house after we were married. Not a hint about that old agreement sleeping in his lawyer's vault. Barry and the lawyer assumed our marriage rendered it invalid. Both were mistaken.

Incompetence!

The lawyer advises me to settle. Miranda's lawyer is expert, her case impregnable. If I fight, the legal fees will devour my share.

I rise to leave but there is more bad news. The lawyer begs my forgiveness. Miranda, pudgy, hopeless Miranda, has a new fiancé – a police officer. She has made wild accusations about Barry's sad and untimely death. The police will be asking questions. Until all is resolved, Barry's assets remain frozen.

I shed a few tears, let the lawyer pat my hand and leave.

Alone in the elevator, I rub my black spot, ready for battle. No need to worry. I had Barry cremated – and quickly, too. But should the police examine my life too closely...

And I want that money. I worked hard for it. It's mine.

Obviously Miranda deserves a violent solution, but the risk is high. I must be wonderfully subtle and effective.

Invisible and inescapable.

Why on earth is my cell phone ringing again? I go to turn it off — I've had enough of that idiot lawyer – but it isn't her, it's my doctor. He must see me immediately.

Now what?

I drop by the doctor's office. He sits me down, begs my forgiveness. He should have taken more care.

On my last visit, his young intern insisted on testing my black spot. It may be my talisman, but it's also melanoma. The tests say it has spread.

Incurable and inevitable.

How apt, you say, the universe has rebalanced. Erased a predator from civilized society. But that's not it at all, sweet heart. The universe really doesn't care about your nice little world.

Sadly it was simply incompetence.

Truly, it will be the death of me.

GLOW GRASS

On a nature walk, we ran across a memorial garden buried in the woods. A perfect gift for a crime writer, a gift that became this novella.

Published in 13 O'Clock, *the second anthology by the Mesdames of Mayhem, Carrick Publishing, 2015.*

Glow Grass *was a finalist for the Arthur Ellis Award for Best Novella, 2016.*

Paula's fists clutched the steering wheel. The cottage, she had to reach the cottage.

Empty fields streamed past her car windows. She searched the deserted highway, desperate for familiar landmarks. Where was the drive-in theatre? Grumpy's gas station?

So long since she last was here. Not since Dad died. The cottage had languished forgotten while she struggled with the wreckage of her life.

She almost missed the drive-in theatre because its familiar sign had vanished. She slowed the Honda and pulled over to the gravel shoulder for a closer look. The drive-in's once-towering screen had collapsed into a chaos of spiky timbers. Half of its *For Sale* sign had blown away.

Told you. Brian's teasing voice jumped back into her head. *Elton is such a loser town, even its doughnut store closed down. It's the biggest dump on Lake Huron. No beach, no museums, no nothing. Time to kill it and put it out of its misery.*

It's quiet, she argued silently. Tourists stay away. That's why Dad liked it.

Sure. Always the contrarian, old Steve. And he threw away a fortune to prove it.

So what? It was Dad's money, not ours.

You know what I used to tell the traders at work? Take a look at Steve North's strategy. Then go be the contrarian of Bay Street's fabled contrarian. Old Steve, the shining icon of zero business sense. Runs in the family, doesn't it, Paula?

Shut up, Brian. I'm an artist, a painter. You know I can't do math.

Separated for nearly two years and Brian still lived in her head. Hour upon hour his dark blue eyes taunted her, while his calm voice outlined her flaws. In detail.

Hey, Paulie, when were you last at the gym? And that stringy hair – time for an overhaul, bunnykins. But, hey, you need good bones, some basics to start with. Ah, forget it. Save your money.

Shut up! She stared through the windshield. When will I be free of him? When?

What if he never leaves my head?

She gunned the engine and bumped the car back onto the highway.

The road plunged on, woods alternating with barren fields. After a long stretch of pines, a weathered white building swung into view. Right at the crossroads where it had always stood: Grumpy's gas station, her signpost to the cottage.

She flicked on her turn signal and drove over the familiar cracked concrete of Grumpy's parking lot. Too late she spotted the rotten chipboard over the windows and the derelict, rusting gas pumps.

So the old fart finally retired. Brian again. *Or maybe he just died from being an asshole.*

Her fingers hurt from gripping the steering wheel. She'd counted on filling up at Grumpy's. Her car was riding on fumes. But the thought of driving ten miles back to Elton for gas felt overwhelming.

I should drive back and gas up. But I have to see the cottage again. I have to make sure it's all right.

The shrill cry of her cell phone ripped through the silence, coupled with a vibration that bored into her side. She fumbled in her jacket and pulled it out. A name flashed on the call display.

Jay, checking up on her.

Again.

I should answer. We need to talk. But not now. I need to be alone.

She shoved the phone back into her thin windbreaker, stifling its nagging cries and gazed at the large muddy field that stretched along the road opposite Grumpy's. A solitary man was driving a black tractor slowly and laboriously over the mangled earth. Old Sark. Still alive. Still farming 40 years on.

He's outlived everybody: Grumpy, Mum, Dad…Maybe he'll outlive me, too.

Hell, I'll risk it.

She tore out of Grumpy's ruined lot and turned down the dirt road that led to the cottage, Lake Huron a blue blur in the distance. Despite the cold spring, green buds studded the bare branches of the bushes lining the road. Soon the thick leaves and weeds would make the woods around the cottage impenetrable.

"And the green grass grew all around, all around. The green grass grew all around."

She chanted her favorite childhood tune as her car lurched down the road. Muddy water filled the potholes to the brim. When she reached the turn-in, her body seemed to sense it before her eyes did, as though it saw her instead of the other way around.

The cottage gate was a slender cedar log stretched over the drive, counterbalanced by a paint can filled with quick-dry cement. She remembered Dad fixing it, the last repair he did before he died.

And not fast enough, Brian loved to say. Then laugh so she wouldn't know if he meant Dad finally fixing the gate or Dad dying.

I remember how bright and clean the gate looked the day of Dad's funeral, she thought. I started crying again and couldn't stop. Only two years ago and now the gate looks like it's been here forever. Things decay so quickly in the country.

She climbed out to deal with the gate, leaving the driver's door open with the engine running. For a quick getaway, Dad liked to joke.

The air felt chill on her skin. Tall pines shut out the sun, everything lay in shade. She longed for the homey scent of wood smoke, a hint to show that other people lived nearby, but all she could smell was mud, wet grass and leaves.

A lilac bush sagged low over the gate. She forced up its heavy branches and peered down the long, narrow drive. At the far end, all she could make out was a patch of silvery green.

Where's the cottage? Why I can't see it?

She heaved the lilac branches aside, hauled up the gate and secured it, the cedar pole slimy under her shaking hands.

The cottage is fine, she told herself. Nothing's happened. If it caught fire and burned down, they'd have called me.

Or would they? And who were "they" anyway?

She shivered and climbed back into the warmth of the car.

No one lives out here except Sark now that Grumpy's gone. And Sark refuses to own a phone. Even if he drove in to Elton to use the gas station's payphone, he'd use Dad's old number. And who would he reach? Brian, not me.

Brian even stole my family's old phone number, she thought. Keeps it for business reasons, he says. And he always "forgets" to pass on my messages. Every time I confront him about it, he just laughs and says he already gave them to me. Ages ago.

Please, please, please let the cottage be all right.

The lilac branches rasped over the roof of the car as she eased it through the gateway. She steered down the overgrown drive, ignoring the scrape of muddy ruts on the undercarriage, her eyes fixed on the green glow of the clearing.

At last, she broke free of the trees.

She let go her breath and turned off the engine.

***

The cottage seemed to shift and shimmer under the trees, its dark brown logs merging with the shadows. The late afternoon sun glinted off an upstairs window.

Silence flowed in through the open driver's window. No birds, no rustle of leaves, no distant murmur of highway traffic.

The cottage watched her, dark, still and vacant.

Her eyes strayed down its east side. The horrible shed was gone. Sark had hauled it away, thank God. Just as he'd promised her the day of Dad's funeral.

Oh, why am I here? I imagined...I thought maybe I'd feel Dad somehow. Now even the air feels empty...

That strange grass, the kind that only grew under the pine trees by the cottage, now filled the spot of ground where the shed once stood. From there, it flowed out to embrace the cottage, indeed to carpet the entire clearing. Spidery and thin-leafed, an unusual pale green, in the dim afternoon light it almost seemed to phosphoresce.

My special grass. My glow grass. That's the green I saw at the end of the drive.

Glow grass? Are you kidding me? The cottage isn't fairyland and you aren't 12. Why don't you do something useful on the internet for once and look up its real name? Get suckers to pay for weeds that only grow under pine trees. Go on, move that fat butt of yours.

I am not fat, she shot back silently. I'm borderline anorexic. The doctor said so.

Her phone rang. She hesitated for a heartbeat, then answered it.

"Paulie, thank God!" Jay shouted over the blare of traffic noise. "I'm standing outside your apartment building. Buzz me in, will you? We need to talk. It's crucial."

Always the drama, Paula thought. Probably why Jay loved being a lawyer.

She roused herself. "Sorry, Jay, I...I had to run an errand."

"You promised you'd stay at home today. You promised you'd call me if you went out, remember?" A rustle as Jay shifted hands. "When will you be back?"

"I don't know."

"What do you mean you don't know?"

"I need some time alone. To think." She listened to Jay gathering breath. "Please don't badger me, Janet."

"Don't call me that."

Janet, Jay's childhood name, simply slipped out from time to time. Paula couldn't help it. "Sorry, *Jay*. What happened with Brian this morning?"

Jay stayed quiet for a long moment. "Look, do you really want to discuss your private affairs while I'm standing out here in the open? Anybody could walk by and overhear us."

"I'm fine with it." Paula worried her bitten thumb nail. "Tell me, how was His Majesty?"

Jay sighed. "Gorgeous as ever. Fit, training for a marathon. But the minute he walked into my office I sensed a change in him, an undercurrent of ...something. Well, you know how hard he is to read, but my intuition says he's weakening."

"Really?"

"Yes, really. He muttered something about feeling worn out by this long, drawn-out negotiation. Then the mask slips back on and he's Mr. Hard-ass. But he's a mere male, Paulie, not tough like us babes. Bottom line: he's handed over a written offer. One we can work with. Finally. But we are still dealing with Brian, right?"

"He wants something."

Jay's hesitation confirmed it. "That's how negotiation works – or doesn't. I admit, that my gut reaction was negative, but then I sat down and did the numbers. And much as I hate to say it, his offer does make sense."

"OK, I'm listening."

"It's complicated. We can't do this over the phone. Where are you?"

Paula didn't reply. She could almost hear Jay bristling.

"Look, I don't blame you for feeling skeptical. We both know how Brian loves to play games, but this time, I believe he's ready to settle."

"He's met someone."

Jay sighed. "OK, yes, but so what? Press your advantage while he's starry-eyed."

"Well, that depends on what he wants."

"OK, fair enough, but tomorrow he could get a wasp up his ass and drag things out another two years."

"Is his new girlfriend rich?"

"Look, forget about her. Sign his damn offer and get on with your life."

"What life? My life's been hell ever since Dad died. My money, my home – everything's gone. Brian made sure of that."

"Let it go, Paulie. Brian doesn't have any money either."

"He's lying! What about that line of credit he ran up against our house — *my* family home — after we split up? The loan that bank manager gave him without my signature even though she knew the house was in both our names. The bank's never been clear on that." For a moment she thought she'd lost the connection. "Jay, are you still there?"

"Yes, I'm still here trying to get a word in. We've been through this a thousand times. You don't have the money to take the bank to court. Your money's gone. That's why we decided to negotiate with Brian. Formal mediation costs too much, remember? Look, everyone loses in a divorce. That's the way it works."

"Then why am I the one who always loses? Brian always wins. Even when he and the damn bank break the law, he wins."

"OK, I'm the first person to admit that our legal system isn't perfect. You're in a dark place. I understand, believe me. Disentangling a marriage can be tough."

"Disentangling?" A worn-out weasel word to obscure the pain and humiliation of divorce, Paula thought. And how would Jay know? She'd never been married.

"Look, try to view your divorce as a life process. You die a little now in order to grow, to become the person you were meant to be..."

Process – Jay viewed every human trauma as a "process".

"Forget it! You tell Brian, no! Absolutely no way! Whatever he wants, it's NO!"

She pressed End Call and flung her phone down on the passenger seat. Roaring the engine back to life, she gunned the car across the clearing.

And immediately lost control. The Honda fishtailed over the wet grass. She slammed on the brakes, slewing and sliding — and slammed head-on into the porch.

Oh, God! Waves of heat roared through her.

She shoved the gears into reverse, but her back wheels spun, whined and failed to get a grip. Jammed up against the porch, she couldn't go forward. She tried reversing again, several times, but the wet grass grabbed her tires like thick mud. The Honda was well and truly stuck — she'd only burn off the last traces of gas trying to get free.

Never pull up to the porch in spring, the ground's too wet. Always park at the end of the drive. For a quick getaway. I should have remembered, Dad.

She turned off the engine and climbed out, sinking ankle deep into the soggy grass.

Now what? She'd cancelled her CAA membership to save money. What about the gas station in Elton? She could call there for help. And pray the staff didn't check her maxed-out credit card first.

Or... she could trek over to Sark's farm. Ask him to pull her out. He was always driving around on his tractor doing some mysterious farm thing or other. She shuddered.

Sark's stoop-shouldered, hulking presence had unsettled her since childhood.

Dad never minded going over to visit Sark or even sharing a shot of rye with him, but she hated Sark's place. It was filled with junk: empty freezers, chains and rags everywhere, cans of oil and jars filled with murky fluids. Everything overlaid with the smell of decay and soiled laundry.

Don't judge him too harshly, Dad would say. He's been that way since his wife died.

But Mum died and you aren't that way, she'd argue. You aren't like Sark at all.

I have you, kid. Sark has nobody. He's alone, buried in his memories. That does strange things to people.

Memories...the cottage lay wreathed in them.

I need to look inside. Then I'll figure out what to do.

She fished the round-headed cottage key from her jeans, went up the porch steps and unlocked the front door. The wrought iron latch lifted with a loud click.

She swung open the door.

And thought, I'm home now. Back with Dad.

***

Dank, moist air rushed over her. I must be the only person in the world who loves the smell of mildew, she thought.

The setting sun streamed in through the open doorway. Slowly the long, plastic-shrouded kitchen table emerged from the dark and beyond it, the shadowy, coffin-shape of the refrigerator, its door propped open.

Step one, turn on the power.

The main floor of the cottage was divided by a fieldstone fireplace, sitting area to her left, country kitchen to the right. The power switch, a heavy black lever on a rusty metal box, rested on the side wall above the stove.

She stepped inside, the dusty plank floor crunching beneath her feet. Almost immediately, the outside light deserted her. She groped her way along the edge of the pine table, the plastic sheet rustling against her thighs. At the far end, she threw out her arms and felt the smooth surface of the electric stove. One hand pressing down on a dead burner, she stretched up and found the switch.

She took a breath and pushed. It refused to budge.

That's my Paulie, skinny little arms but plenty of fat in the can.

She braced both hands on the stove and jumped. Shoes sliding on the slippery enamel, she scrambled up. A burner cracked loudly under her knee. Using both hands, she threw her weight and rage against the switch. And felt it clunk into position.

Nothing. No power.

Now what? No power meant no heat, no light, no hot water, no stove... Had she forgotten to pay the cottage hydro? No, the bank paid the bill directly out of her account. But what if the bill had arrived during one of the many times her funds had run dry?

I've got to get some light in here.

She grabbed the roller blind over the window beside the stove and pulled. With a huge clatter, the blind flew out of her hand, ripped free of its mountings and crashed down onto the floor.

Grey light filtered in through the dusty windowpane. She slid down off the stove and picked up the fallen blind. Dead insects littered the floor, the plastic sheeting, everywhere she looked.

God, that's disgusting. Never mind, step two, turn on the water. Don't need electricity for that.

She dumped the blind on the table and went over to the sink by the far wall. The inlet tap connecting the cottage's water system to Sark's well rested in the cupboard beneath it. She crouched down, opened the cupboard door, grabbed the inlet tap and tried to turn it. The bloody thing wouldn't budge.

She leaned her forehead against the open cupboard door, sweat beading on her brow. I have to do this, she thought.

She groped through the darkness of the cupboard for Dad's wrench. Mum always needed it to turn the water back on.

Found it! The jaws of the wrench slid perfectly over the nut at the base of the tap. She breathed in, pushed down on the wrench and felt something give.

A familiar hiss and clanking in the intake pipe. Air rushed out of the kitchen tap in the sink above her head, followed by a belch of foul-smelling water. She stood up, feeling light-headed. Rusty water gushed out of the tap, but as she watched, it began to run clear, flushing two years of dirt and debris down the drain.

I did it!

She left the water running and dropped the wrench on the counter by the sink.

Now to get some light and fresh air in here. I feel like Pip in *Great Expectations* tearing open Miss Havisham's apartments. I've come, come to let the light in!

She moved swiftly from the sitting room to the back bedroom to the cramped bathroom tucked behind the kitchen, raising blinds, fumbling with the rusty catches on the windows, hauling up their heavy frames and propping them open with the wooden sticks Dad had cut so long ago. They still bore his handwriting in black crayon: back bedroom left, back bedroom right...

Dad's cottage exactly as he left it. How easy to pretend he was out by the beaver pond cutting trails. Or off to Elton for groceries.

Yeah, Elton's King Tut and his dump of a tomb.

That's enough, Brian. You've always hated the cottage.

She rubbed her arms and retrieved the wrench to get water flowing in the toilet. Retracing her steps back to the kitchen, she glanced up the narrow stairs that rose behind the stone fireplace. Her old bedroom lay up there in the loft with her favorite toys. But with the power out, all she could see was darkness.

Funny how Dad always slept in her bed upstairs whenever she and Brian visited. Switching places, kid, now that you're married, he'd say. You two take the master bedroom out back.

Hoping for the grandchildren that never came, she thought. I'll look upstairs later once I get the power back on.

She dropped the wrench beside the blind on the table and turned off the taps. How much better to *act* instead of sitting around. She'd been drowning in thoughts since Dad died.

Out in the car she could hear her phone ringing. She ignored it.

I'll get a fire going in the fireplace, she thought. Boil some water and make a cup of tea. Dad always left tea bags in the cupboard. I'll eat that chicken sandwich I couldn't finish at lunch. Tonight I'll sleep on the sofa in front of the fireplace and pretend that I'm camping. Come morning, I'll walk the ten miles to Elton's gas station. I can do it. That's all I've been doing lately, walking and thinking. Endlessly.

She ran her hand over the rough fieldstones of the fireplace, remembering when Dad and Sark built it, their grunts of effort as they lifted the stones and mortared them into place. The cement for its base spread out like a strange moist cloth. And the repellant yet magnetic scent of their sweat.

Charred pieces of wood rested in the grate, remnants of the fire Brian built during their last, dreadful visit.

I'm throwing those ashes into the woods as far as they will go.

She jerked open the mesh curtains of the fire screen. A loud snap. A piece of wood struck her shoulder. She jumped, stifling a cry.

A mousetrap!

She glanced at the copper box holding the firewood. Another trap lay half-buried in the logs, a small mummified form caught under the rusty metal spring.

I hate those traps. They're so cruel.

Mice are vermin. They bring death on themselves.

She unhooked the little brass shovel from the stand holding the fire irons and slid it under the trap. Trying not to look at the dead mouse, she carried the trap outside. At the edge of the woods, she swung the shovel in a wide arc and heaved everything into the bush.

Done.

She breathed in the chill evening air. When had Brian put out those mousetraps? The day of the funeral or the day of the accident? She remembered nothing but chaos from that day: ambulance, police...and in the laneway, Sark sitting silently astride his brush cutter...She rubbed her cold hands.

Dad dies and you find time to set out mousetraps? You're sick, Brian.

Hey, you and Steve always complain that I never do anything at the cottage. Can't have it both ways.

Where else did you hide traps, you jerk?

On the road down to the lake the growl of a faraway engine. She tensed. A car? No, too rough. It sounded like heavy machinery. Farm machinery.

Sark!

He had an uncanny way of knowing everything that happened at the cottage. And she sensed that he liked her knowing that he knew. Sometimes a faint smile would steal across his face – she'd notice it though Dad never did.

Dad always maintained that Sark didn't have a bad bone in his body, but she dreaded his sealed silence — and the oppressive obligation she felt, whenever she ran into him, to make one-sided inane conversation until she devised a lame excuse to escape. His sly smile would creep back then, too.

The motor sounded much closer. Definitely a tractor.

Turning into the cottage drive.

***

He'll realize I'm here alone...

She ran down the eastern side of the cottage away from the drive, her mind working. I'll head up to the beaver pond while it's still light, she thought. Wait him out.

The trail to the beaver pond started behind Dad's shed. She had no choice now, she had to cross over the horrible spot. A shimmering tongue of glow grass leaked out into the trail as though pointing the way to the pond.

Fire shovel in hand, she dashed over the sinister spot and plunged down the narrow track into the safety of the trees. The path snaked deeper into the forest, the glow grass dwindling out behind her.

The beaver pond lay buried in the woods half a kilometer north of the cottage. At one time, homesteaders owned a farm there with an apple orchard — or so Sark had told Dad. But the settlers had departed long ago and over time their log house had crumbled into the forest soil. The orchard had grown wild until beavers dammed the creek that cut through the forest, drowning the apple trees, turning their dead trunks silver.

The lost farm made Dad melancholy. It reminded him of time's passing, he said. But in the beaver pond all she saw was life: frogs, dragon flies, turtles, snails and minnows. Once a pair of Canada geese nested there. Another time she even caught a perch, which Dad cooked for dinner. She'd always meant to find out who owned the land around the beaver pond. All Dad could tell her was that it lay well beyond their property line.

The trail suddenly veered right, not left. She stopped, bewildered, faced with a tangle of brambles and reeds

The path turns left here, she thought. Dad cut the trail along the *left* side of the pond so we could walk along its edge to the far end. Too many cedar trees on the right side: Dad never owned the heavy tools he needed to cut through them. I've used this trail since I was a kid. It turns left here, not right

She clutched the fire shovel as though she could beat her memory into submission.

Oh, God, this divorce is driving me crazy.

Crazier, wouldn't you say?

Go away, Brian.

She took the path to the right.

It led into the shadows of the now-towering cedar trees. A short distance along, she spotted a soft green light: glow grass growing into the trail.

It spilled out from a tiny track that branched away through a clump of alders. Dodging the leafless bushes, she followed it into a small clearing.

There a stone garden bench rested in a soft carpet of glow grass. Several small stones bordered its circular edge. On closer inspection, the stones proved to be store-bought garden ornaments, inscribed with a single word like "Forever" or "Remember". Between the stones stood small plaster statues of angels holding soiled plastic flowers or soggy, bedraggled ribbons. One angel held a glass engraving of the poem, *Desiderata*, the relic cracked and damaged by the weather. Votive candles in red glass holders lay scattered among the stones, most burned down to the end.

This was a memorial garden. But for whom?

She sank down on the bench. The tiny monuments were cheap — she'd seen them for sale in dollar stores. None bore a date or name. Perhaps the strange garden was an amateurish, heartfelt tribute to a family pet.

But what if it wasn't?

She shivered. Who built the garden? Why hide it in the woods away from prying eyes? Was it the unknown owner of the beaver pond?

Over the years, she and Dad had found evidence of strangers around the pond: cigarette butts, fish line and hooks, empty beer cans... Anyone could pass through their cottage property when she and Dad weren't there.

The mysterious gardener had taken glow grass from the cottage and replanted it here. That felt like a warning, a challenge even. As if the unknown gardener was telling her, *You abandoned the cottage. Now it's mine to do with as I like.*

The woods were deathly silent. Yet she had an uneasy sense that someone lurked in the shadows. Watching, waiting, matching her breath for breath. She felt in her jacket for her phone and remembered she'd left it in the car.

She stood up slowly, wielding the puny fire shovel. Saw nothing but lifeless bushes and dark cedar trees.

Heart pounding, she stumbled back to the main trail. She walked briskly, faster and faster through the waning light until she was running flat out. She didn't stop until she burst clear of the trees.

The porch light was on. Under its harsh light, the glow grass had turned a chalky, sepulchral white.

Sark stood on the front porch, his bulky form blending into the dusk.

***

He sensed her presence, turned and stared in her direction. She shrank back against the cottage wall.

Slowly, laboriously, he lumbered off the porch. Stood there without speaking, the hard bones of his face sculpted by the evening shadows.

She had no choice, he'd seen her plain enough. She stepped forward.

"Hello, Mr. Sark." She gripped the fire shovel, held it close to her side. "Thank you, um, thank you for clearing away the shed." She gestured feebly at the spot behind her.

He grunted.

"I see...I see the power's back on."

"Weren't out. It's yer switch."

"My switch...Oh, but I turned it on." She cursed the defensive tremor that crept into her voice.

"Gone rusty. From sitting around. It's the damp what does it. Had to work it but good." With a gnarled fist, he motioned turning the black breaker switch off and on.

"You were inside? You went inside my cottage?"

"Wet kills a place." He took off his flat grey cap and ran a huge hand over his bald scalp. "You selling?"

"What?" Had he really said that? "Um, no, I-I' m not selling. Not now. I'm…I should say *we*, dropped by. To make sure, you know, everything's still all right."

"Long time."

"Yes, it's been very emotional." Under his stare, she struggled to find a simpler word. "Hard."

He nodded. Settled the cap back on his head.

"I see that Grumpy's gas station is gone."

Something stirred in the deep-set dark eyes. A slight shift in the heavy shoulders. She'd forgotten how large he was, how he towered over her even now as an elderly man. He gazed at a point past her shoulder, waiting, listening. She felt helpless. Maybe mentioning his old enemy, Grumpy, had been a mistake.

"I'll be going now." He nodded and trudged toward the mouth of the drive, cutting a dark line through the glow grass. She watched his hunched form turn down the road and vanish into the twilight.

Where was his tractor? She could have sworn she'd heard it turn into the drive.

She rushed over to her car and retrieved her phone. Her hands shook so badly, her fingers slipped on the touch screen.

He was here. Inside. My. Cottage. He knows I'm alone.

She punched out Jay's number.

No ring. Nothing.

Instead the phone uttered its inanely happy call tone and turned itself off. The outline of an empty battery flashed on the screen.

Out of power.

The sound of a vehicle on the drive. The phone slipped from her hands, bounced back onto the passenger seat.

He's coming back. He's coming back!

She stared, blinded by the oncoming headlights.

***

A car door opened. Someone called her name.

"Jay?" Had she heard right? "Oh, thank God, it's you!" Paula didn't know whether to laugh or cry.

Jay appeared from behind the open driver's door, her red cashmere coat swinging, her arms full of groceries. Paula rushed over to hug her.

Jay laughed, extricated herself. "What's going on? You look like a scared rabbit!"

"Sark was here. He knows I'm alone." Paula felt abruptly, chillingly sick. "You must have driven right past him on the way in."

"No, I did not see Old Psycho McDonald."

"He was here just a minute ago. How could you miss him?"

"I don't know. Hey, relax, will you. What were you planning to do? Beat him to death with that silly little shovel?"

The shovel felt slippery in Paula's sweaty grip. Sark wasn't the only one who could make her feel like an idiot. "How-how did you find me?"

"How long have we known each other? 20 years! Think about it: we met in Grade Six when we were 11. Here, take these groceries, will you? My arms are falling off." She pushed the heavy bags into Paula's arms. Tossing her oversized Prada handbag over one shoulder, she headed back to where her Mercedes stood idling.

"Jay, wait! Leave your car on the drive." The driver's door slammed shut. "Don't! Wait!"

The noise of the V6 engine drowned out Paula's words. The Mercedes churned through the wet grass, heading directly toward her. Paula staggered under the burden of the groceries, barely sidestepping out of the way. With a spray of mud and grass, Jay skidded to a stop inches from the Honda's back fender.

"Why don't you listen?" Paula shouted as Jay reappeared. "You nearly ran me over!"

"What *are* you talking about?" Jay locked her car with a beep of her electronic key.

"The grass is too wet. My car got stuck. Now we're both trapped!" Paula stumbled over to the porch and dumped the groceries on it with a loud clank of bottles.

"Hey, take it easy! I bought us some decent Merlot for once." Jay bounded up the porch steps and flung open the front door. "Phew, I'd forgotten the awful mildew smell in this place. I never could understand why your dad loved this old dump so much. With his money, why didn't he invest in Muskoka?"

They both knew the answer: Dad avoided the rich outside of work. Farmers and working men were the folks he admired. Why he loved that Jay, the scholarship student, became Paula's best friend at school. She remembered Dad telling her, "Jay's father is nothing but an old drunk. Let's give that girl a real family."

"Earth to Paulie: bring in the groceries, will you? Before the damn raccoons eat them."

"Hold on a minute. We need to talk."

"That's why I drove out here." Jay charged ahead of her into the dimly lit cottage.

It occurred to Paula that Jay didn't merely move through the world, she bored through it, light and air fracturing around her. Or so it seemed. In fact, ever since their childhood, it had always seemed so.

Paula trailed after her, lugging in the groceries. Nowhere clean to set them down. Even in the faint light shed by the wagon wheel chandelier, the insect bodies littering the plastic sheeting looked disgustingly obvious. Jay hadn't noticed the bugs yet, intent as she was on her cell phone. She'd dumped her precious Prada bag on the encrusted table. And her red Armani coat.

She'll freak, Paula thought. She hates bugs. I should dig out the vacuum cleaner and disappear every last one of those little buggers. But Sark...I want to get out of here.

Her legs were trembling. "Can you forget about your job for one minute? Please call the CAA."

"What did you think I was doing?" Jay frowned, staring at her phone. "There's no signal in here."

"But you got through to me earlier. Maybe it's your phone service. Try my phone instead." But her phone was out of juice, lying outside in her car, Paula remembered.

Jay made a gesture of frustration. "Never mind. I'll walk out to the road and try there."

"No, don't! Not with Sark around."

"Hello, he lives here. On the farm next field over."

"Will you listen for once? Sark was here. He was here *inside* the cottage."

Jay stared at her. "Why did you let him in if he scares you so much?"

"I didn't let him in! He walked in like he owned the place when I was out in the woods. He told me so to my face!"

"What were you doing in the woods? I'm confused."

Paula took a deep breath and blurted out her story, her words tumbling over and over each other like a rock fall: the stuck switch, the overgrown trail, the strange garden...

Jay frowned. "OK, that's creepy. Maybe Old Psycho McDonald thought he was being neighborly. Out here in Braindead, Ontario, nobody locks their doors. People walk in and out of each other's houses all the time. Country crap."

"No, when Dad was alive, Sark always knocked first. Don't you see? He walked in here because he *knew* I was alone!" Paula realized she was shouting.

"Oh, for God's sake! If Sark was going to rape and murder you, he would have done it already."

"Thanks a lot."

Jay held up a hand. "OK, OK. If you insist on talking about psycho farmers and weird graveyards in the woods, I need wine. Where did you put the groceries?"

Paula pointed to the spot by the table.

Jay reached down and gasped, "Oh, my God!" She snatched up her coat, brushing it off frantically. "Nice of you to tell me about the dead bugs before I dumped my new Armani on them."

"Sorry." Paula tossed the wrench and the broken blind under the table and peeled off the plastic sheeting over it. She took great care to wrap up the dead insects inside the plastic. At a loss when she was done, she shoved the rolled-up bundle under the table as well.

Jay banged an oversize bottle of red wine down on the counter. "I can't remember where your dad hid the wine glasses."

Paula pointed to the cupboard above the sink. She watched Jay extract two wine glasses and grimace at their dusty interiors. She took a breath. "You don't believe me about that strange garden, do you?"

Jay frowned while she rinsed the glasses under the kitchen tap. "Well, you do tend to exaggerate just a little. Goes with being artsy, I guess."

"My being an artist has nothing to do with it! I know what I saw."

"Relax, I'm just teasing you." Jay shook the excess water out of the glasses. "Look, your mystery garden is a leftover from Hallowe'en. Teenagers having a party. More country crap." She unscrewed the metal cap on the bottle. "Come on, don't stand there freaking out. Go build us a fire. It feels like the inside of an aquarium in here."

Wordlessly Paula picked up the shovel from where she'd dropped it next to the groceries and made her way over to the fireplace. Light beamed down from the brass floor lamp over the worn brown sofa. She sank down into its chilly cushions, twisting the fire shovel handle in her fists. Time to come clean with Jay. She should have done it right after her meeting on Monday.

I hope we're still friends afterwards, she thought. But if we aren't, well, maybe it's time to move on. For both of us. When we were kids, we were the school rejects, so we had to stick together. But we're so mismatched, we always have been. Jay's always been the pretty one, tall and athletic, while I'm the short, dumpy one who failed gym. She's the super bright math whiz, but I only had A's in art. So much has happened since school: Jay's a lawyer with a big Toronto firm. I got married and divorced. Well, I'm trying to get divorced.

"How's that fire coming along?" Jay shouted from the kitchen.

"I'm working on it." Paula bounced off the sofa and kneeled down next to the wood basket.

I'll burn you to nothing, she thought, glaring at the charred wood in the grate. Cleanse the cottage of you. And you with it, Brian.

Hey, our marriage is over. No need to get violent.

I wish you were dead. I wish you were dead instead of Dad.

Ooh, I am so scared. What are you going to do, bite me?

She reached for the kindling in the wood basket and hesitated.

You scared of another dead mousie? Go on, dig deeper. See if I left another surprise, you scared little bunny.

I'm sick to death of you and your traps. Go away!

She yanked kindling and logs free of the basket and threw them on top of the ashes. Standing up, she reached for the green biscuit tin where Dad stored the matches. But when she tried to pry the lid off, it wouldn't budge.

"Jay, I need your strong fingers."

Jay appeared, a full wine glass in each hand, her Prada bag slung over her shoulder. She set the glasses down on the mantelpiece and dumped her bag on the floor.

"Cheers!" She grabbed the nearest glass and flashed Paula a broad smile, showing off her brilliantly bleached teeth.

Sensing Jay's eyes on her, Paula picked up the other wine glass and took a sip of Jay's "decent merlot". The dark red wine tasted strangely sweet, but with a faint under taste.

"What's the matter? Don't you like it?"

"It's OK." Paula took a second sip to keep things pleasant. There it was again, that off-putting, almost metallic flavor.

"Let's get down to business." Jay dropped down on the sofa and patted the sofa cushions. "Come, sit down."

"First tell me what Brian wants. And be up front with me this time."

"I'm always up front with you."

"Answer my question!" Paula banged her glass down on the mantelpiece. Wine slopped over the brim.

Jay shrugged and sighed. "He wants the cottage."

Gotcha, Paulie.

***

Paula's throat constricted. Surprise had rendered her speechless.

"I know, I felt the same. Outrage, disbelief." Jay waved her wine glass. "But look at what this place costs you: there's property tax, insurance, water and power, plus your car and the gas to drive up here. And that's not counting repairs. You can't even begin to cover the costs on the pittance they pay you at the art gallery."

Paula stared into the dead fireplace. Jay was right – the cottage bills had eaten through her slender savings. And the nasty letters from the county tax office were getting nastier.

"Would giving up this place be so bad?" Jay went on. "It's falling apart. You haven't been up here since …well… since your dad's accident. To be honest, I thought you'd *want* to be rid of it."

Paula wiped her eyes. "You don't understand. It's all I have left of Dad. And he didn't die in the cottage. He died out in the shed."

So much blood, it looked black not red. Splattered over the garden tools, leaking through the wooden floor, soaking into the grass beneath it… the glow grass. She hadn't understood what she was seeing when she opened the shed door to look for Dad. Her mind couldn't process the horror. A severed femoral artery, the medical examiner said. Your father tripped over the garden scythe. She remembered crying, But Dad was always so careful with his tools...

Jay looked subdued. "I'm sorry, Paulie. I shouldn't have stirred up those bad memories."

Paula found her voice. "You know, I never thought I could hate anyone. I mean, truly hate someone. Brian's always despised the cottage. He only wants it now because he's figured out a way to get money for it."

Jay shrugged. "Makes sense."

A cold gust of wind blew in through the open back window. Paula rubbed her arms. "That's why Sark asked me if I was selling when he was here. Brian cut a deal with him. Probably told him it was a sure thing."

"Maybe you're right. So what if Brian cut a deal with Sark? Who else would buy this swamp pit? After all, Sark's the one who sold it to your mum and dad in the first place."

"Dad said Sark needed the money." Paula rubbed her forehead. "Sark's poor. He's always been poor. He could only pay Brian a fraction of what the cottage is worth."

Hey, money's money. The cottage isn't an asset, it's a liability. Time to trim the fat.

Go to hell, Brian. The cottage isn't yours to sell.

Yet. You'll cave, bunnykins. You always do.

"Sark's got a thing about land." Jay drained the rest of her wine. "Remember how he moaned to your dad that Grumpy stole the gas station land from him? And Grumpy always called Sark dumb as a pail of hammers. Well, guess who owns the gas station now? Sark!"

"How do you know that?"

"I got curious when I saw Grumpy's was gone. So I stopped and called my assistant. Got him to check the land registry."

"What happened to Grumpy?"

Jay shrugged. "Maybe Old Psycho McDonald ploughed him into the back field."

"That's not funny. When Sark was here, I told him I'd never sell. I thought I was reassuring him. Instead he's going to be furious."

Jay slammed down her empty glass. "So what do I tell Brian?"

"Tell Brian…" Paula clenched her fists. "You tell Brian I'll burn the cottage to the ground before he takes it away from me."

"Now you're being unreasonable."

"No, I'm not." Paula picked up the matchbox tin again and forced her nails under its lid.

"Look, I can't spend any more time on you and Brian. I'm in big trouble with the firm. If I don't bill a ton more hours, they'll fire me. Just sign Brian's damn offer and move on."

"No, I said no and I meant no." She wrenched on the lid. "You never listen, Jay, that's why I have to tell you…"

The tin exploded in her grip.

Clumps of black matter showered down over the hearth. A strange powdery dust drifted through the air, settling over the scattered match sticks.

Paula looked down and screamed.

***

"There – there was something in the tin." She forced herself to look. Saw feathers, claws… "Oh, God. I think…I think it's a burned bird."

Jay bent over the fallen matchsticks. "You're right, it is a bird. Well, that's gross." She grabbed the brush hanging with the fire irons and began sweeping up the fragments.

"A pair of swallows used to nest in the eaves outside the back bedroom. They came back year after year. I loved them…" Paula leaned her forehead against the cold, rough stones of the fireplace. "I know who killed the bird and put it there."

"Your Brian obsession is getting tired." Jay pushed the black remnants into a little pile.

"He built the fire last time."

"Enough about Brian!" Jay picked up the fire shovel from the floor by the sofa. "Look, a bird got caught in the chimney when you had a fire. It could have happened any time. Maybe your dad put it in the match box to bury it."

"Are you crazy? Dad believed what the Navahos believe, that death poisons everything it touches. He and Mum bought that tin on their honeymoon. It was special to him. Now it's spoiled forever."

"Oh, come on! Going mental over a cheap old tin." She made to toss the bird fragments into the fireplace.

"Wait, stop!" Paula grabbed her arm. "Throw it in the woods. The tin, too."

"OK, fine. But after this, I want more wine. And since you don't like the stuff I opened, let's try the other bottle I brought. It's got a cork, so we'll need your corkscrew."

"OK," Paula murmured.

She watched Jay brush the bird's ashes into the fire shovel, grab the matchbox and carry everything outside into the night.

Cold sweat trickled down her back. Her stomach burned. She thought back to the watery chicken sandwich she'd bought at the gas station on her way out of Toronto. And Jay's sickly sweet wine.

I think I'm going to be sick…

A faint noise, a creaking overhead. She looked up. A soft thud, as though someone had dropped a book. Directly above her head.

Someone's upstairs!

Sark!

Hey, I always thought Old Psycho McDonald liked you, Paulie. I mean, really liked you.

Helpless, she gazed up to the steps to the loft. Shadows smudged the stairs. Darkness hovered at the top of the landing.

Sark crept back through the woods. That's why Jay didn't see him. He climbed in through the open back window while we were outside...

She couldn't breathe. Couldn't move.

A car door slammed. The sharp crack of sound unfroze her legs. She stumbled, tripped and blundered her way outside.

A faint mist hovered over the glow grass. The fluorescent blue of Jay's cell phone screen floated in the dark beyond the cars.

"Jay," she managed. And then louder: "Jay!"

Jay materialized from the darkness, swishing through the mist like a ghostly surf, the fire shovel swinging in her free hand. She shoved her phone into the back pocket of her tight-fitting designer jeans.

Paula staggered down the porch steps. "There's someone in the cottage." She tried to keep her voice low, looked back over her shoulder.

"No way!" Jay's dark brows, such a contrast to her shining blond hair, pulled down in a deep frown.

"It's-it's Sark!"

"No, it can't be. Listen!" Jay pointed down the drive.

Faintly, in the distance, the unmistakable growl of a tractor. Revving back and forth. Driving over the black muddy field the way she'd seen him when she first arrived.

"Jay, we need to leave. Right now."

"Make up your mind. Is Old Psycho McDonald inside or outside?" Jay brushed past her, bounded onto the porch and disappeared back inside.

I am not imagining it, Paula told herself. She needed her phone. With the cottage power back on, she'd recharge it.

She rushed over to passenger side of her car. And felt a crunch underfoot.

***

No! It couldn't be!

She dropped to her hands and knees, groping through the wet grass. Impossible to see in the dark. Her fingers struck something hard. She felt a sharp jab of pain.

Glass! Even in the dim porch light, she could make out the bloodied fragment in the grass.

Biting back the pain, she combed through the grass. In a few moments, she'd retrieved the shattered pieces of her cell phone. She'd stepped on it, crushed it beyond repair.

But I left it on the passenger seat. How could it have slipped out of my car?

"Are you going to sit out there all night?" Jay called from the cottage.

Paula forced herself to stand up. She opened the passenger door and tossed the remains of her ruined phone inside.

"Have you calmed down now?" Jay was looking out the front door.

"I'm fine." Paula clutched her bleeding hand. "I really did hear a noise upstairs."

"Fine, you heard something," Jay snapped. "Probably a mouse. This swamp pit is a rodent highway. Are you coming back in or not? I'm starving."

Paula made herself climb up the porch steps. It's only a mouse, it's only a mouse, she chanted under her breath. She eased in through the front door.

"Will you stop muttering to yourself?"

'I'm fine, Jay. Let's eat. I'll open the wine." Action was better than thinking. Action would calm her nerves.

She walked over to counter and pulled open the cutlery drawer where Dad kept the corkscrew. She reached in blindly.

And heard the snap of a mousetrap.

***

Hot tears ran down her cheeks. She tried to free her hand from the drawer. It was caught.

"Jay…" she gasped against the fierce pain. "Help me."

Jay rushed over. "What's wrong with you?"

"A mousetrap. Pull the drawer out."

Jay seized both sides of the drawer and heaved. Nothing happened.

"Yank it out all the way." Paula's breath was coming in gasps.

Jay hauled on the drawer again. It wrenched free of its slide and crashed to the ground, sending a glittering cascade of knives, forks and spoons skittering across the floor.

"Holy hell!" Jay grabbed Paula's arm making her wheeze in pain.

Paula stared at her injured hand in the trap. With a strange objectivity, she thought, My finger doesn't bend that way.

"Hold still." Jay's strong fingers bent back the shiny copper hinge of the trap. "Now! Hurry! Pull it out!"

"I-I can't."

"Do it! I can't hold it open."

With a savage tug, Paula twisted her finger free. A vicious snap shot the trap from Jay's grip.

Paula clutched her left wrist. Her finger refused to move. It was already darkening and swelling. "I-I think it's broken."

Jay looked pale. "I'll get the first aid kit. You still have it, right?"

Paula nodded. "Please hurry."

Jay disappeared into the bathroom.

I call that sweet irony, don't you? Broken marriage, broken ring finger.

I hate you, Brian! A shining bolt of pain shot down her left arm.

Jay returned, carrying a battered metal box with a red cross on it. The old first aid kit Dad had used to patch up their childhood scrapes.

Must think...Paula's finger throbbed in agony. Jay made a splint for it with an emery board and some ancient gauze. But no aspirin inside the first aid kit.

Paula stumbled over to the side fireplace and leaned against the stones. She might as well tell Jay now. Anything to take her mind off the pain.

"Jay, I...please sit down. We need to talk."

Jay slouched down on the brown sofa, twirling the fire shovel. "OK, I'm listening."

"I owe you so much. You were the friend I turned to when Dad died and Brian took off." Paula gathered her breath. "I couldn't think straight after finding Dad like that. And losing the house, Dad's money gone. Brian turning ugly...the stress was crushing me."

Jay frowned. "So what's the problem?"

"Trying to negotiate with Brian has been a disaster!"

"What are you talking about? We're done! I have the papers with me. Sign and Brian's out of your life forever."

"No." Paula shook her head. "He's relentless. He'll never stop."

"It's because he wants the cottage, isn't it?"

Paula straightened up. "Well, that certainly made up my mind." There was no easy way to tell Jay other than to say it. "I've been doing a lot of thinking lately. I...I went to see Michael Rothstein on Monday."

"What!"

"He's the family lawyer who's always in the news."

"I know who Michael "Barracuda" Rothstein is." Jay picked up the fire shovel, twisting its handle between her hands. "You're unbelievable! Wasting everyone's time lawyer shopping. Thanks a lot, 'best friend'!"

"It's my life, Jay."

Jay threw her a hard look. "The Barracuda will tell you exactly what I've told you a thousand times already: you don't have the money to take the bank to court."

"Mike thinks I have an excellent case."

"Mike?" Jay pulled a face. "Of course, he'd say that. Do you have any idea how much The Barracuda charges per hour? You'll spend the rest of your life paying off his legal fees."

"He's offered to do it *pro bono*."

"You heard what you wanted to hear. The Barracuda never does *pro bono* work."

Paula cleared her throat. "You wouldn't necessarily know this, but Dad and Mike's father were in school together. Mike's father was the poor Jewish kid there on scholarship, so the other boys gave him a rough time. Dad stuck by him. Mike says his dad never forgot that. He wants to help. He's offered to handle my case personally...and now I've decided to say yes."

"You...you're *firing* me?"

"Yes, I'm really sorry, Jay. I should have gone to see Mike in the first place." Paula tried to ignore the throbbing pain in her hand. "Negotiating with Brian seemed like the best way when you suggested it, but he's fooled both of us."

Jay stared into the cold fireplace in stony silence.

"Don't you see? You, Brian and I...we know each other too well. You knew him before I did. Remember how you introduced us at the golf club? That's the problem. He's manipulated both of us."

"You're crazy!" Jay squeezed the handle of the fire shovel so hard that Paula thought she could see it bend. "You want to blame Brian for everything that's wrong with your life. None of those therapists helped you. No one can."

"I'm sorry I dragged you into my mess. I asked too much of our friendship, Janet."

"Don't you call me that!"

The shovel clanged against the stones of the fireplace, inches from Paula head.

"Did you just throw that at me?"

Jay stalked off into the kitchen.

Well, that went horribly, Paula thought, heart churning.

"I need a drink," she heard Jay mutter. Then louder, "Where the hell did you throw the corkscrew?"

A loud clatter as Jay scooped up the fallen cutlery from the floor and dumped it back into the kitchen drawer. The white-hot pain from Paula's broken finger was blurring out the world. "Jay?" she ventured.

"What do you want?"

"Do you have an Advil in that big Prada bag of yours?"

Jay sighed with drama. "Fine, you're in luck. Go sit down. I'll bring it."

Relieved to restore the peace, even for a moment, Paula turned to sit down on the sofa. That's when she saw it: a tiny pinpoint of blue light winking at her from between the sofa cushions like a snake's eye.

With her uninjured hand, she reached down and found Jay's cell phone. It had slipped out of the shallow back pocket of Jay's slender-fitting jeans.

She swept her finger across the phone's screen to unlock it.

A message appeared: "Keep her busy."

The message was from Brian.

The world stopped.

***

The pop of a cork broke the spell.

The shattered pieces of Paula's world kaleidoscoped back into a new, chilling reality. Jay and Brian. Working together.

The proof rested in her hand.

Her throat had dried up, her heart was beating so wildly she could barely breathe. She slipped Jay's phone into her jacket.

She edged around the end of the stone fireplace and peered into the kitchen. Jay stood by the pine table, turned away from her. Though slender, she possessed a light athletic strength.

Brian's equal in every way. Especially in deceit.

Think, I must think.

Paula watched Jay fill their glasses with a murky red wine.

How could you do this to me, Janet? she thought. Dad called us spirit twins. He paid your way through law school, so you'd never be poor again. It can't just be because of the money. It can't just be because you and Brian wanted all Dad's money.

But of course, it could. Dad had always told her that money made people crazy. He'd seen too much in the brokerage business. People did unspeakable things for money. To strangers, friends and family. Especially to friends and family.

She'd asked Brian again and again for the financial documents, the hard copy proof that Dad's money had vanished in the recession, only to be told by Jay that she'd never be able to decipher them. Because she couldn't do math.

But Jay could. And she had the legal knowledge to funnel Dad's stolen money to an off-shore account.

"You're muttering to yourself again." Jay turned to face her, a glass of wine in each hand.

Paula met her gaze, but kept still.

"Here, drink this." Jay held out a glass.

"Alcohol won't help the pain." Paula's mind was whirling.

"Best cure there is." Jay dug through the front pocket of her jeans. "And take these."

Paula stared at the two elongated green capsules in Jay's hand. "Those aren't Advil."

"Advil won't help a broken finger. My sports doctor prescribed them when I tore my hamstring. Go on, take them and drink up."

"You're not supposed to mix alcohol and painkillers."

"I am beyond tired listening to you whine. Take them or I'll shove them down your throat!"

"What's wrong with you!"

"What's wrong with me? You went to The Barracuda behind my back, wasted two years of my professional time, got me in big trouble with my law firm for not billing enough — and you're asking me what's wrong?"

Paula's eyes strayed to the front door. She had to get outside. But Jay was standing between her and the door.

"You're not drinking." Jay took a gulp of wine, her eyes never leaving Paula's face.

Paula motioned with her bandaged left hand. "I only have one hand." She squeezed past Jay to the opposite side of the table.

Nothing now between her and the front door.

She took the pills from Jay. She made a display of shoving them in her mouth. Praying they wouldn't dissolve, she picked up her wine glass.

Heart beating, conscious of Jay's ever watchful eye, she drew in a mouthful of wine. She pressed the pills hard against her bottom teeth with her tongue, a trick she'd mastered in childhood to avoid swallowing medicine.

"You're not drinking."

She had to swallow now. She downed as little as possible and choked. Coughing and spluttering, she doubled over. And spat the pills into the wine.

"What the hell are you doing?"

To cover, she drew in a rasping breath. "Took too big a drink."

Jay wasn't convinced.

Paula straightened up, pasted on a smile and took another sip, curling her fingers tightly around her glass to hide the pills in the depths of the blood-red wine. "There, that's better." She smiled again. "Much better."

Jay took a swallow of wine. Said nothing.

She had to distract Jay. Her mind ricocheted from one idea to another. She cleared her throat. "That illegal line of credit on our house that forced me to sell..."

Jay made an impatient gesture. "Will you stop? Brian got caught in the recession, OK? He made some bad choices. Give it up. That money's gone, it's never coming back."

Paula closed her eyes, persevering. "You and I know what the bank did. But we should have been asking *why*."

"This is pointless. I'm not your lawyer anymore."

"Mike knew why right away."

"Oh, really?"

Paula licked her lips. "I felt so stupid when he pointed it out. The answer's obvious: Brian had sex with the bank manager."

Jay clutched her wine glass. "That's not possible."

"Why? Because she's married and 20 years older than we are? Brian held his nose and did the necessary, as he puts it. He's always used sex to get whatever he wants. I should know! He couldn't get Dad's money with just a little sex. But if he married me, he'd get it *all*."

"Believe that if you want. And if you keep repeating that idiotic lie about the bank manager, she'll sue you. And *she'll* have 'an excellent case'." Jay mimed the quotation marks with her free hand.

Paula felt a prickle of heat in her throat. She had to convince Jay, she had to. "Oh, Brian did her all right. Big time. Mike's junior did some digging. Finding the proof turned out to be easy. Mike told me this morning. I felt so upset, I had to get away. That's why I drove up here to the cottage."

"I don't believe you!"

"Why? Every woman we know wants Brian. *I* fell in love the minute I saw him. I'd never met anyone that good-looking. I thought he was a movie star when you introduced us." Her limbs shook with a chill foreign to the damp in the cottage. "He had at least three affairs while we were still together. And they weren't just one-night stands."

"You're making this up!"

"Brian told me himself. Rubbed my face in it. And those are only three affairs I know about."

Jay said nothing, her expression unreadable.

"Don't you remember? I asked you about infidelity when Brian took off. In a general sort of way. You said adultery doesn't count for much nowadays even in divorce court." She took a step back from the table, feeling dizzy. "I never told anyone, not even you, because I felt so humiliated."

"You're lying."

Paula shook her head. "I wish I were." She set glass down on the table. "Do you really think Brian will stay with you once he has all my money?"

"SHUT UP!"

Jay's glass shattered on the log wall behind Paula. The acrid scent of spilled wine filled the room.

A loud crash from upstairs stunned both of them.

No mistaking that for a mouse.

***

Paula ran for the front door. It wouldn't open. She wrestled madly with the latch. Heaved her weight against the wood, her terror obliterating all sense of pain.

"It's locked," Jay said behind her.

Paula turned to face her.

"Let me show you the key." Victorious, Jay dug through the back pocket of her jeans. Her smile died. "Where is it? Where's my phone?"

Paula shook her head, refused to speak.

Jay stared, realizing. "*You* took it." She grabbed the wine bottle from the table. "Give it to me!"

"NO!"

"Give it to me or I'll smash your finger to a pulp!"

The open back window! Paula plunged past her, but Jay latched onto her like a wild animal. She caught hold of her hair, yanking, twisting and pulling.

Paula screamed, desperate to free herself. She flailed out with her good arm. Jay hooked her ankle, threw her off balance. A horrible sensation of falling. An agonizing thud down onto the dusty floor.

Then Jay was straddling her, weighing her down, pummeling her unmercifully. She screamed again, frantically fending Jay off with her good hand, but all she struck was air.

A glint of light. A flash image of Jay raising the wine bottle.

White-hot agony burst through her broken hand.

She couldn't cry out, the pain was so great. She retched.

"You little bitch!" Jay scrambled off her.

Paula rolled over. Foaming acid liquid roared up her throat and splattered over the floor. Splashed onto Jay's jeans.

Jay raised the wine bottle, a glass baseball bat, aimed at her temple. Paula lifted her limp arm — a ridiculously puny shield.

"Stop playing around, you two!" someone shouted.

Jay froze in mid-swing. Paula coughed through a haze of anguish.

Brian had left her head and re-entered the real world.

He was upstairs in the cottage.

***

Jay leaped up. "*You* stop playing around! Get your ass down here and help me with her!"

Brian laughed. "Listening's more fun."

Jay swore and stomped over to the stairs, wine bottle in hand. "I'm tired of doing all the work."

"But you do it so well. And hey, Jay-bird, you told me you could handle this. Sounds like you lost it."

"Get down here!" When Brian didn't reply, Jay reached over and flicked the light switch by the back bedroom door. It controlled the light up in the loft.

Nothing happened.

"What did you do to the light?" she shouted.

Brian chuckled. "Come up and find out."

"Is she lying about the bank manager? Those other women? Tell me she's lying."

"Hey, Paulie doesn't have the brains to lie. Like her old man that way.'

"You bastard!"

"Aw, you're so cute when you're mad."

Jay charged up the stairs, clenching the wine bottle.

Now was her chance. Paula tried to stand up, but her legs buckled beneath her. A deadly lethargy had invaded her body. She dragged herself onto her hands and knees. The window… she had to get to the back window.

She retched again, bringing up the dregs of Jay's drug-laden merlot.

Upstairs Brian and Jay were arguing in urgent, intense bursts. The world was fading. She shook her head violently. If I pass out, I'll die.

"Hey, Paulie," Brian called down. "Come up here and play. We're waiting."

"Who were those women? Tell me!"

A thud and a crash. "Cut it out, Jay." Another crash. "I said cut it out!"

"Tell me!"

Brian swore. "I just tripped over your damn toy box, bunnykins."

A blue iridescent light cut through the upstairs darkness, strobed back and forth across the landing at the head of the stairs. So Brian had a phone, too.

Paula fought to hang on to consciousness. Jay had been texting Brian all along. They must have driven up together. Jay probably dropped him off at the end of the cottage drive. He could have slipped in unseen any number of times.

Suddenly Jay let out a cry of rage. Brian shouted back. They were getting physical. Splintering the upstairs furniture.

The world was growing dark. Paula dragged herself over to the kitchen table — the only hiding place she could reach. She crawled underneath it, grappling with the bug-infested plastic sheeting. The noise of the fight upstairs drowned out the ghastly rustling sound it made as she burrowed in next to it.

With her undamaged right hand, she extracted Jay's phone from her pocket. Punched in 911 with her thumb. It rang and rang.

Please pick up, please pick up!

"Emergency services. Fire, ambulance or police?" a faint voice said in her ear.

"Police! *Police!*" Paula shouted against the din of the rampage upstairs.

"Stand by." The dispatcher's voice died out. He must have put her on hold.

Answer, please answer.

Shrieks and blows overhead.

Why didn't the police answer? She stared at the phone screen. Only half a reception bar. So Jay hadn't lied about the poor service after all.

A thunderous thump from upstairs. Glass shattered.

Silence. They'd stopped fighting.

The bing of Jay's phone sounded unnaturally loud.

A message appeared: Call lost.

***

"Hey, bunnykins," Brian called down.

Her heart beat like a trapped bird. The police tracked emergency calls, didn't they? They'd track her call to the cottage, wouldn't they?

But even if they did, it would take too long. They'd arrive too late.

"I'm losing patience, sweetie."

She pulled herself onto her knees. Her legs trembled. She had to get out. She had to get outside or she would die.

"Who the hell keeps Ninja Turtles when they're over 30?" Brian said. A horrible crunch followed. "Hey, that was fun."

He's trying to lure me out. He's counting on me to be weak. But I will not let him kill me!

"Got a whole toy chest to play with up here. Better come up and stop me."

Go to hell, Brian! She refused to utter a sound. She would not be drawn.

"Bye, bye Snow White," Brian said. Glass and china smashed.

She wouldn't think about her beloved toys, she wouldn't.

"Bye, bye Mickey Mouse."

Blue light flashed through the gaps in the planks of the ceiling as Brian worked his way through the loft. Destroying her precious memories one by one.

Paula wiped away her tears with her good hand.

The stairs creaked. Someone was coming downstairs.

Through the maze of table and chair legs, she spied Brian's trim, muscular form on the steps. He was dressed in his running gear: black tank top, black shorts, black and gold-trimmed running shoes. No sign of Jay.

"I know where you're hiding, Paulie. Bad things happen in showers."

He vanished into the bathroom. She heard the plastic shower curtain rip. And the clang of the shower hooks as they hit the tub.

The bathroom window banged shut. She jumped, smacking her head on the underside of the table.

"I heard that." He was standing outside the bathroom door. "Come on out. Make it easy on yourself."

She dared not breathe. He dove into the back bedroom. A huge clatter as he heaved aside the wooden sticks propping open its only window. He crashed it down. Glass splintered.

Oh, Dad, help me.

Her knee knocked against the fallen kitchen blind. She reached for it with her good hand.

And found the wrench.

She watched him leave the back bedroom. He headed for the open back window next to the fireplace. Her last chance of escape.

She wrestled free of the plastic and hauled herself out from under. She tossed the blind onto the table. Clinging to its edge for support, she pulled herself up onto her shaking feet. Only the kitchen table stood between them.

"There you are, little mousie." He turned and flashed her an engaging smile. Who would believe he was about to kill her?

She kept her uninjured right arm close to her side... "Stay where you are. Don't come near me."

He sauntered over. "How'd you like my traps?"

"I thought Jay set the traps."

"Not her style. No sense of humor. Had to work fast while you and Jay-bird were outside. Except for the swallow in the tin. Did that the day of old Steve's funeral."

He stepped closer. "Clever girl, Jay-bird. Learned lots of tricks in law school. Except the whole 'drain the assets, hide the money offshore' thing took so damn long."

"Where is she?"

He shrugged. "Taking a break. She's played her part."

"She drugged me."

He threw out his hands. "Hey, makes sense you'd off yourself in your crappy childhood dump, crying for dear old Dad. After all, you're not the most stable person, are you, bunny brain?"

"Fuck you, Brian."

He'd reached the other side of the table. Behind him, the blackness beyond the back window beckoned. "You know, you could have sucked down that nice merlot and gone to sleep like an old cat at the vet's. A sofa cushion to the face to make sure and a soft exit from your pathetic life. Now you force me to improvise. I'll have to burn down this swamp pit." His face brightened. "But hey, there's an upside to everything. You kept up the insurance. Jay-bird checked."

He lunged for her. Batted the blind off the table like a scrap of paper. It clattered to the floor.

She wheezed in fear. No need to act.

"God, you're a pain. Tell you what." He clapped his hands in a theatrical gesture. "I'm going to string you up on this chandelier thing." He gestured at the wagon wheel above the table. "I'm going to make it nice, slow and painful. Let you catch your breath, pull you back up." He flashed a boyish grin. "Make you last all night."

"Why…"Her voice died, refused to come out.

He crashed his fists on the table, making her leap in shock. "Because you won't cooperate!"

She found her voice. "Jay, don't do this. We were friends once, best friends. Answer me, Jay. Where are you …Where…?"

Water hit her forehead. She swiped at it with her injured hand. The gauze on her broken finger turned scarlet.

She felt a drop on her cheek. And another.

A red rain was leaking through the gaps in the ceiling planks. Skittering over the table top, dropping down on her...

And hitting Brian, too.

A strange, humid smell. Not rain: Blood!

He killed her. He killed Janet!

She screamed in horror – and that saved her. Distracted him for a heartbeat as he jumped the table.

She swung the wrench. Crunched it against his cheekbone.

He roared in pain and outrage.

She ran for the window. He scrabbled after her.

She was halfway through the window when his fists seized her. She struck out again with the wrench, fighting and screaming. He got it away from her.

A gleam of metal in the tumult of their fists. Brian yelled and grabbed his head. The fire shovel bounced onto the floor.

A voice shrilled at her to run. A nightmare vision stood on the stairs. Sodden with black and red blood. Holding a broken wine bottle.

Brian threw himself at the phantom. They grappled for the bottle in a deadly tug of war.

Paula rolled over the window sill. Tumbled into the wet grass.

And charged blindly into the woods.

***

The moon was up. The glow grass shimmered all around her with a chill white phosphorescence. Mist rose from it like smoke.

She ran mindlessly. Her shaking legs moved with a will of their own. The pain in her hand dwindled to a distant thing.

I must not fall. If I fall, he'll kill me. Must get into the trees. Hide in the dark.

The turn-off to the beaver pond loomed before her. She could hear his footsteps on the path like a cold wind behind her.

She dove into the darkness under the cedar trees. The track to the hidden garden shone like a silver thread.

Must hide. *Must hide.*

The moon shone down on the empty garden bench, bathing the tiny angels and stones in an eerie pattern of light and shadow.

He'll find me.

She fought her way into the woods, struggling through a ferocious tangle of bushes. Branches and thorns scratched her face. She could penetrate no further. Already she could hear the huff of his breath on the trail.

She dropped to the ground. Huddled to make herself small.

A mad thrashing of bushes – he was coming down the track.

"What the hell!" He'd found the garden. "You build this for dear old dad, bunnykins? It's tacky enough."

She peered through the web of undergrowth. Moonlight outlined his head and bare torso. It glinted off the broken wine bottle in his fist. Black matter stained its gleaming edges. He'd made short work of Jay.

"I know you're in here."

She held her breath. She dared not move.

No one out here in the depths of the woods. Her cries for help would die out as they did for all prey.

He was circling the garden now, peering into the shadows. Suddenly an intense brightness flooded the woods. His cell phone!

He stood by the stone bench, beaming its light over the undergrowth. A fiendish beacon, searching, probing.

She pressed her pale face hard against her knees, squeezing down even smaller. To be one with the dark.

"You're making me very angry." His voice sounded too close. "You really don't want to do that."

She sensed the light moving away. A quick glance showed him sitting on the bench, phone in one hand, broken bottle in the other. His foot bounced in annoyance as though she was late with dinner. Or boring him.

"I'll find you when the sun comes up. Getting cold here, waiting around. Tell you what. Come out now and I'll make it quick."

He paused, thinking. What was he doing now?

She sensed a vibration. A light shone through her pocket. The phone: he was calling Jay's phone!

She yanked it out and heaved it into the trees. Its throbbing techno-beat ring sounded as loud as a jet plane. It landed too close to her, its blue light pulsing through the brush.

He was on it in an instant. Foraging through the weeds and bushes like a wild dog. He was so close she could smell his acrid sweat. One more step and he'd land on top of her.

She broke free of the bushes. Landed in the garden.

The glowing track had vanished. She ran for it anyway. And smashed into a wall.

A terrible force caught hold of her. She struggled madly. Felt her jacket rip away. She tried to run. The stone bench struck her knees. She fell heavily.

Brian loomed over her. She screamed in icy terror.

He slashed down with the wine bottle. It shattered on the bench in a glittering mass of shards.

She couldn't escape the glass, the darkness, his rage…

He uttered a wet cough. Strangely he'd grown a second smile. His hands clutched his throat. A black fountain gushed over his naked chest.

He toppled onto his knees beside her.

She struggled away from him. He threw her a beseeching look. Reached out his hand.

And fell to the ground, shaking in a lethal seizure, twitching and shuddering, as his life's blood emptied into the glow grass.

Her breath had left her. She could only watch, paralyzed.

A piece of the darkness detached from the woods. A shape as big as a mountain. The moonlight shone down on a pale and pitted face. Gleamed on the scythe in his fist.

Sark!

His huge hand reached for her. Gathered her up. Pressed her against his stony chest. She smelled wet wool and earth.

"You all right?" his hoarse voice asked.

She burst into desperate, gulping sobs. They tore out of her, the way the blood had gushed out of Brian. "You-you killed him!"

"Like a hog. Done lots in my time."

"You …saved me."

"Swore to Steve I'd look out for you." He kicked Brian's now flaccid leg. "This one needed killing."

She tried to contain her crying. "He-he killed my friend Jay."

"She weren't your friend. She was with him."

So he'd heard everything through the open windows. She'd sensed him out there, lurking, listening.

"Brian killed Dad. He set a trap for him in the shed. I know he did it but I'll never be able to prove it."

"Your dad's blood made the grass grow."

"Wh-what?"

"His spirit makes the grass shine."

She backed away from him, wiping her cheeks with her good hand. "You built the garden. You made it for Dad."

Sark nodded his massive head. "Steve was a good man." He wiped the scythe on the leg of his overalls. "I'll clean up the mess. They won't bother you again."

"What-what will you do?"

"Back field needs ploughing."

She wanted to tell him to stop. That they must call the police. But the strength that had saved her was ebbing.

"You selling?" His hard dark eyes met hers.

"No, never." The glow grass in the track shone like the sun. She edged down it. "The cottage is yours if you want it. Take it! Take it back!"

She fled down the trail. All around her, the glow grass shimmered with an unearthly light.

She ran down the trail, skirting the spot where the shed once stood, passing the dark hulk of the cottage and the two cold, useless cars parked end to end. She ran and ran. Down to the end of the drive and up the road to the highway.

Her lungs burned. Somewhere during her wild flight, she'd lost her shoes. She hobbled over the dirt road in her bare feet, fear and pain beyond her.

A faint greenish light rimmed the eastern horizon. Dawn was breaking.

Grumpy's abandoned gas station was flooded with a red light. A police car stood idling on the cracked concrete.

With a cry, she staggered toward it and collapsed. Car doors opened, footsteps ran toward her. Two police officers bent over her.

"You-you found me," she stammered.

Their kind hands lifted her up. And she felt the daylight embrace her like her beloved glow grass.

THE LIZARD

This story began when a friend told me about her daughter's new pet, an animal the daughter wasn't looking after properly. It started life as flash fiction for Maureen Jenning's course on creativity, then grew into a longer story.

Published in Crimespree Magazine, *Summer Issue 2013 and reprinted in* Kings River Life Magazine, *August 2014. Also reprinted in the 2014* Bloody Words *program book, the final year for Canada's national crime fiction conference.*

Winner of the Bony Pete Award for Best Short Story, 2012.

Margaret sat alone in the vet's examining room, clutching the empty cat carrier the way she'd held Mr. Kim in his blanket.

All over now. Death was so simple, so complete. Why did she still fear it when it seemed the most natural thing in the world?

The young technician came back into the room carrying a pamphlet. She began explaining the different options for pet memorials. If Margaret wanted to be certain that she'd have only Mr. Kim's ashes in the urn, instead of commingled pet remains, the cost would be far greater.

"Please, I can't think of this now." Margaret's tears flowed with a will of their own. She hated crying, had hated crying ever since she was a child, but she felt powerless to stop.

Flustered, the technician fetched the vet. He was a grey-haired, soft-spoken man about Margaret's age. Gently he touched her arm.

"There's no rush. You can let us know later today."

She accepted the tissue he handed her and wiped her cheeks.

"Mr. Kim was lucky to have you," the vet went on. "Medicine couldn't help him anymore. You did the right thing, Margaret. I would have done the same for my cat. Think of it as the last kindness you could do for him. Would you like some help getting home?"

"No, no, I'll be fine. I didn't drive today because...because I knew I'd be upset. But I'm better now. I'll be fine." She stood up, cat carrier in hand, and left.

The outside world hit her in a torrent of light and noise. The cold spring wind cut through her red wool coat, but she didn't head for home. Instead she crossed the road and boarded the streetcar heading east. She took a single seat by the window, balancing the empty carrier on her knee, thinking of the long ride ahead. Ultimately it would be a futile journey like all the others, but she banished the nattering advice of the social workers from her mind.

The street car lumbered away from her familiar middle-class surroundings. Tall trees and brick homes gave way to the glass and stone of the business district where her late husband once worked. Later, beyond the city core, the street car plunged past bleak concrete buildings and dirt-filled yards. She watched for a particular configuration of pawn shops, pay-day loan arrangers and dollar stores. When it appeared it startled her, though nothing on the street had changed.

She pushed the request stop button, breathed to calm herself, and stepped down from the street car into a dusty, seemingly deserted world.

I shouldn't have worn my red coat, she thought. *I stand out enough as it is.* She slung the strap of her purse over her shoulder and pressed the bag against her side with the cat carrier. *Walk with purpose,* she thought and crossed over the road to the sidewalk. *Don't make eye contact. If anyone talks to you, don't answer, whatever you do.*

Jennifer's apartment building had acquired a new patina of graffiti. Margaret recognized a black scrawl next to the entrance. A gang tag, one of the social workers had told her.

The lock on the glass entrance doors was broken — as it had always been. The same sharp odor of mildew and sewage lingered inside the lobby. The battered metal mailboxes had deteriorated though — only a handful had doors now.

"Those boys smashed my mail box." An elderly lady sat hunched in a wheelchair by the elevator, her shapeless feet shoved into a pair of fuzzy blue slippers. "Now I gotta sit here so's I can get my welfare check. Damn super won't do a thing. Damn cops won't come here no more. Them gangbangers do what they like and the hell with everybody else."

Margaret had to lean past her to push the button for the elevator.

"Can I see your cat?" The old woman craned her neck to peer through the carrier door. "I can't see it. Hold still so I can see. I can't see nothing. Where's your cat?"

"He's hiding," Margaret shifted the carrier to her other hand. Hurry up, hurry up, she urged the elevator.

She heard the front door whoosh open. Two men strode in. The husky, shorter one wore a black leather jacket heavy with metal studs. The other much taller man had stretched a strange rubber mask over his head.

The old lady clutched Margaret's arm. "That's not the boys. Don't know those two."

Margaret's finger ached from pressing the call button. Had those men followed her in from the street? She hadn't noticed them outside, but then she wasn't equipped to.

"Hey, lady, you're trespassing, you know that?" the short one said.

Margaret stared at the closed elevator door, heart pounding.

"Go away," the old woman shouted. "I want to see her cat."

The tall one stepped closer. Margaret swallowed. She saw now that his mask wasn't a mask at all: elaborate black and red tattoos covered his face and naked skull.

"Hey, you deaf? We're talking to you," he said.

"I-I was showing her my cat," Margaret said.

"I don't see it." The old woman rattled the carrier. "Take it out and show me."

The tattooed man sneered. "That's right, go ahead. Take it out. Show us, too."

The elevator arrived. Margaret bolted inside and hit the button for the fifth floor. Nothing happened. She stared helplessly at the men through the open door.

"Leave me alone. I just want to see my daughter. She lives here. Please, leave me alone."

The short one grabbed the tattooed man's forearm. "Chill, man, she's here to see her kid. We got other business." He nodded to Margaret. "It's OK. Go on up."

Slowly the elevator door began to move. The old lady stared at Margaret through the closing gap. "Is your cat a ghost?"

"Yes, yes, that's right. My cat is a ghost."

Finally, blessedly, the door closed. The elevator jerked into motion. Margaret collapsed against the back wall, her face running with sweat. *Thank God,* she thought. *Oh, thank God.*

The elevator creaked up to the fifth floor and shuddered to a stop. A fresh current of fear rushed through her. What if those men followed her upstairs?

She scratched the plastic side of the cat carrier in her haste to force her way out past the sluggish door into the hall. She ran down the ragged carpeting to Jennifer's apartment.

Jennifer looked pale and sweaty when she opened her door to Margaret's frantic knocking. "Oh, it's you."

"Please, Jenny, can I come in?"

"Sure, fine, whatever." The girl vanished into the gloom of the hall.

Margaret slipped inside and made sure the door was locked behind her. She set down the cat carrier and unbuttoned her coat, waiting for her heart to slow, breathing in the familiar, pungent odour of marijuana, sweat and decayed food that was as much a part of Jennifer and Paul's apartment as its four walls.

The cramped living room was its usual filthy shambles except for a large glass tank resting on the battered coffee table. Jennifer sat slouched on the torn sofa beside it, her dark blond hair greasy, her pink track suit stained.

Margaret sat down beside her. "Please be careful about opening the door, Jenny. Promise me you'll always ask who it is first. It was only me this time, but there were some strange people downstairs…"

"God, how long did it take you to start this time? One second, that's all! Just tell me what you want and get out." Jennifer kicked the coffee table with her bare foot.

"Where's Paul?"

"Out."

She should have noticed. The apartment was mercifully silent. Other times she couldn't make herself heard over the thump of rap music and the incessant ringing of Paul's cell phone. He used a ridiculously incongruous ring tone, the Teddy Bears' Picnic.

If you go out in the woods today...

"This is new." She pointed to the tank. Inside an iguana rested on a bare tree branch. It looked like a miniature dragon, its skin an intricate green mosaic. "It's so beautiful, Jenny."

"Uh-huh." Jennifer rubbed her dry lips.

"I've heard that iguanas are very intelligent," Margaret pressed on. "You can teach them tricks and things. Where do you put its food and water?"

"Paul says it can go months without anything."

Margaret doubted that was true. "When is Paul coming back?"

"I don't know. I thought you were him. I can't stand this waiting around. He said he'd be right back." Jennifer scratched her bare forearm. It was dotted with what looked like dark insect bites.

Oh, God, Margaret thought. Many of the sores were crusted and oozing. She dared not confront Jennifer about them, at least not yet. Instead she studied the lizard, its wise wizened face and strangely human limbs. "Your pet's back leg looks twisted."

"It got broken."

"How did that happen?"

"It just happened. Stop asking questions. That's all you ever do, ask questions."

Jennifer and Paul had smashed an aquarium during one of their fights. Margaret remembered finding the fish stuck to their carpeting like pale, gelatinous jewels.

The iguana stirred. Its hind leg flailed and slipped off the tree branch.

"I'm worried about your pet," she said. "It seems to be in pain. It can't move its leg properly. Why don't I take it to my vet and let him take a look?"

"Forget it!"

"I'll pay for the vet."

"How much?"

Margaret shouldn't have mentioned money. The social workers had warned her never to mention money in front of Jennifer.

"How much would you pay? How much have you got with you?" Jennifer's eyes shone with a frightening hunger.

Margaret fumbled in her purse for her wallet. "Here's 50 dollars. That's all I have with me."

"50 bucks? That's it?" Jennifer snatched the bills and shoved them into the waistband of her sweatpants. "That's no help."

"When was the last time you ate something?"

"I'm fine. Leave me alone." Jennifer bounced off the sofa and ran over to the window. She parted the dusty slats of the venetian blind with her fingers to look out. "God, Paul, where *are* you? You said you'd be back right away."

How could Paul have such a hold on her daughter? He was years older, sickly thin from his life on the streets. He reminded Margaret of a furtive wet mole.

"How long has he been gone?" she asked.

"All night." Jennifer chewed her thumb the way she used to in grade school. "He told me to sit tight and keep the door locked. That he'd take care of the problem."

"What problem?"

"Business." She looked at Margaret. "If you really want to help, give me 50,000 dollars."

"What! Paul owes someone 50,000 dollars? What happened?"

"He screwed up, OK? Happy now? Quit asking me questions. Since you don't want to help me, get out."

"Jenny, please. I don't have 50,000 dollars to give you. Even if I did, we both know it wouldn't change anything. There will always be a next time with Paul. And a time after that."

"Well, this time he's dead. And I'm dead, too."

"Jennifer! You know I'd give you everything I have, every cent, if it would get you out of …out of all this."

"You'd love me to move back home with you, wouldn't you? That's why you came here today, isn't it? You never stop trying. You'd do anything to get me away from Paul. Well, it's never going to happen. I won't leave Paul. I'm never leaving Paul." She paced back and forth in front of the window, pausing every few seconds to look out.

"Give me your phone." She held out her hand for it.

Margaret looked around. No land line. Paul's cell phone was Jennifer's only link to the outside world and he had taken it with him.

"Give it to me!" Jennifer lunged for Margaret's purse. She rummaged through it and pulled out the phone. Tossing aside the bag, she rushed into the bedroom, jabbing at the phone's touch screen.

Margaret picked up her purse from where it had fallen. She sat listening to the click of the lizard's claws on the tree branch as it fought to keep its balance. It stared at her through the glass, its dark eyes full of sorrow. *What should I do?* she thought. *God help me, I don't know what to do.*

"Paul's not answering." Jennifer charged back into the living room, the phone in her fist. "His phone keeps going to voice mail. Why isn't he answering?"

"Maybe...maybe he's on the subway." Or maybe he recognized my number and doesn't want to answer, Margaret thought.

"I know what you're thinking. You're thinking he took off. Well, he'd never leave me. He loves me. And I love him. He said he wants us to die together."

The phone rang in Jennifer's hand.

"You see! That's him. That's his number." She pressed the phone to her ear. "Hey, Paul..."

An instant later she dropped the phone as though it had scorched her hand. "It's them. It's those men. They want the money." She collapsed on the sofa. "Where's Paul? What's happened to him?"

Hands shaking, Margaret retrieved the phone and ended the call.

"Do those men know where you live? Answer me, Jennifer. Do they know where you and Paul live?"

"I don't know. Paul's real careful, I'm careful, but..."

Margaret's throat had gone dry. "We need to leave. Right now. Go on, get your jacket."

Jennifer shook her head. "No! I'm not leaving without Paul."

"We can't wait for him. Please, listen to me just this once."

Jennifer didn't move. She stared blindly at the lizard.

How do I get through to her? Margaret thought. *Oh, God, please help me.* "Sweetheart, do you know why I came to see you today? Did you see the cat carrier? I came here because of Mr. Kim."

"What about Mr. Kim?"

"I-I'm so sorry. Mr. Kim had a tumour. I kept him at home with me as long as I could, but he was so weak and miserable...I couldn't bear to watch him suffer any longer. I took him to the vet this morning."

"You put him to sleep. You killed him!"

"Jenny, that's not fair. You know how much I loved Mr. Kim."

"You liar. You *killed* him!" Jennifer buried her face in her hands, sobbing madly, gasping and gulping for air.

"Do you really believe I wanted him to die? Even the vet said I did the right thing."

But Jennifer wasn't listening. She cried desperately until her sobs subsided into a soft coughing and sniffling.

"What did the vet do with his body?" she asked.

"He's keeping it at the clinic until I ...until we decide what to do."

"OK." Jennifer wiped the tears off her face with the sleeve of her sweatshirt. "I want to bury him at home. In the garden."

"Yes, let's do that. Let's go get Mr. Kim." Margaret touched her daughter's shoulder. "And we'll take your iguana with us and get its leg fixed."

"OK." Jennifer stood up and walked calmly into the bedroom.

Margaret collected the cat carrier from where she'd left it by the front door. She lifted the glass lid off the iguana's tank and gently curled her hands around its body. To her surprise, its skin didn't feel cold, but soft and dry. It didn't resist when she lifted it out and slipped it into the carrier on top of Mr. Kim's blanket.

"Weird cat." Jennifer had returned, wearing Paul's old leather jacket over her sweat suit. She threw Margaret a weak smile and picked up the cell phone from where it rested on the coffee table.

They left the apartment and walked down the hall to the elevator.

Margaret pushed the call button. "There were two men downstairs when I came in. They scared me. If they're still in the lobby, I'll talk to them. I want you to pretend you don't know me. Walk straight out of the building, run to one of the stores and use my phone to call the police. Can you do that, Jenny?"

Jennifer nodded.

They rode down to the lobby in silence.

The doors opened. Margaret nearly dropped the cat carrier. The two men were standing directly in front of the elevator, leaning over the old woman in her wheelchair.

No way to push past them without a confrontation.

"Give me my check, you bastards," the old woman shouted. She swiped at the brown envelope the tattooed man dangled out of her reach. "I told you which floor and which number, now give it to me. Give it to me!"

Margaret sensed Jennifer edging away from her. She took a deep breath and stepped forward. "What's going on?"

"Mind your own damn business." The tattooed man flashed her a look so piercing it nearly made her stumble.

"Bastards!" the old woman shouted again.

"Please, don't tease her. She's old." Margaret watched Jennifer hurry past the wall with the broken mailboxes, her head down.

The short one shrugged. "Give it up, man. Give her the check."

The tattooed man let the old woman snatch it from him. "That sure fixed your memory, didn't it, you old bitch?"

"God'll getcha. God'll get all of you." The old woman wheeled herself out of the lobby.

Margaret started toward the outside door, but the tattooed man seized her arm.

"Hey, lady, you're rude, you know that?"

"Sorry, I-I didn't mean to be. My cat's sick. I have to take him to the vet." She forced herself to stare directly into the man's hideous face. "Would you like to see him?"

"Sure, show us the damn cat," the short one said.

The tattooed man released his grip on Margaret. She held up the cat carrier so that he could look inside. She watched Jennifer swing through the outside doors.

"That's not a cat, you crazy bitch," he said. "You're a freak, you know that?"

"You're right," she said. "You're absolutely right. I'm crazy. And you're right, it's not a cat, it's a lizard."

Jennifer wasn't running for help – she had pulled out the cell phone.

Margaret's arms were shaking with the effort of holding the carrier. "My lizard is hurt. It needs to see a vet. Can I go now?"

Jennifer was punching numbers into the phone.

The short one smiled. "A lizard. That's cool. I kind of like that." He nudged the tattooed man. "Come on, leave her alone. We've got business upstairs."

Margaret heard a faint, familiar ring tone when they shoved past her into the elevator:

If you go out in the woods today...

The elevator door closed, choking off the rest of *The Teddy Bears' Picnic.*

Margaret rushed outside. She tore the phone away from Jennifer with her free hand and hurled it into the street. The oncoming street car crunched it into splinters on the rails.

"What did you do?" Jennifer cried. "You're crazy!"

Margaret shouted and waved to get the driver's attention, dragging Jennifer with her. Thankfully, he stopped.

They climbed on board. Jennifer wiped her eyes and dug out one of the bills Margaret had given her to pay their fare.

Margaret's legs refused to hold her any longer. She collapsed into the seat behind the driver. She dared not look out the window for fear she'd see the men running after them. Jennifer slumped down beside her – she insisted on holding the carrier on her lap.

Margaret could scarcely breathe during their trip back into the city. Even when they reached the safety of downtown, her heart was beating like a wild thing.

"Paul..." Jennifer said. "Why did those men answer? Where is he?"

"Paul can't answer. He's gone."

"He can't be."

"Let's think about Mr. Kim now. One thing at a time."

Margaret closed her eyes and took her daughter's hand. *I'm doing the right thing,* she thought. *It's the only thing I can do.*

But she wished someone would hold her the way she'd held Mr. Kim that morning.

THE ULTIMATE MYSTERY

This cross-over tale was my first foray into speculative fiction. It stemmed from an idea that had nagged me for many years.

Published in World Enough and Crime, *Donna Carrick ed., Carrick Publishing, 2014.*

Finalist, Derringer Award, Long Short Story, 2015

"Mother, why is it always so hot in the tunnels?"

"Because that's how the Goddess made the world, Lily. Now get back to work." Maria resumed her digging.

Lily sighed. Her earliest memories were of shifting earth and rocks. Now, as an older child, her labors had become as automatic as breathing. She knew little else.

Luckily the guards had assigned her and Maria to the outer tunnels. To be sure, this meant they were the lowest level of digger, but it also meant that they mostly labored in solitude. The heat there felt less oppressive and they could steal time to rest. Except for the infrequent inspections, for the most part the guards left them in peace.

These periods of solitude gave her and Maria time to talk. For Maria had always been there, large, forbearing, ever-patient under Lily's barrage of questions. Early on Lily had asked her, "Are you my mother?"

Maria sighed. "Not exactly. But, yes, for all intents and purposes, I am your mother."

"I don't understand. If you are not my mother, who gave birth to me? Where did I come from?"

"We all come from the same place. From The Centre at the heart of our citadel. We are all birthed there."

Lily had learned from the other diggers that all the tunnels of the citadel converged underground at The Centre, the place where the Authorities and their chief, the Supreme Ruler, dwelled. Only diggers of the highest rank carved and maintained the tunnels close to The Centre. Few, if any, of their companions had seen it.

"But where is my mother? I want to see her. I want to be with her." When Maria replied that was not possible, Lily pushed down her fears and asked, "Did something bad happen to my mother?"

"Perhaps. I don't know. We are all separated from our mothers at birth. None of us will ever see our mother."

"Why not?"

"Because that is The Law of our world."

Maria warned Lily once more that she must never call her "mother". If the guards sensed the two of them had grown close, they would separate them. Their relationship must remain a secret.

Instinctively, Lily knew better than to press Maria for more answers. No one dared to question The Law. To do so meant a summons to the Authorities at The Centre, and those diggers never returned.

∗∗∗

Miriam looked out her kitchen window, searching for Lucy. Where was that child?

"Lucy!" she called, striding onto the deck. The garden looked terrible in the summer drought, full of bare dirt patches, weeds and insects everywhere. A perfect match for the falling-down house they'd rented from the old farmer.

"Lucy, it's time for lunch."

She spotted her daughter's white blouse in the field beyond the garden. What was she doing? Digging again. Endlessly digging for buried kingdoms and treasure. What an imagination Lucy had! Well, no help for that. There was so little for her to do out here on the plains, having no one to play with.

"Lucy!" She watched her daughter toss away her stick and trail back toward the house. Almost 11 years old. Old enough to be told, her husband had said.

Miriam folded her arms. *I don't care if the Bible says I must obey him in all things,* she thought. *For all intents and purposes, I am her real mother.*

Lucy climbed onto the deck. "Mom, it's so hot. I hate this global warming. Why can't the scientists do something about it?"

"Because the scientists are wrong. They don't understand that God made our world. Even this awful heat is His will. Now, wash your hands and come for lunch, like a good girl."

***

Lily rarely saw diggers her size, since children fared poorly in the tunnels. Many died because they did not get enough to eat. During the frequent rock falls and tunnel collapses, children were more likely to lose their lives. Often, when she and Maria picked their way through the aftermath of a catastrophe, she'd see small limbs protruding from the debris.

More disturbingly, she'd heard stories about guards taking young ones to the Supreme Ruler. In the dark, the other diggers whispered that those children simply disappeared. The guards had their way with them. Then ate them.

She asked Maria if this was true.

"Of course not," Maria replied. "If we uphold The Law, the Authorities take care of us. That is the social contract our ancestors made long ago. We work to support the Supreme Ruler and the Authorities – and they feed us and keep us safe."

Which really means we dig and dig for nothing, Lily thought. Their food consisted of chunks of matter heavily processed at The Centre. On rare occasions it tasted sweet, but other times it tasted foul and bitter. Her fears multiplied.

"Is there meat in the food?" *Children?* she wanted to ask.

"No, not for diggers like us," Maria replied. "Only the privileged eat meat. Meat keeps them strong so they can take care of us."

In other words, the Authorities and the guards ate meat. But so did the hunters who left the citadel to forage for food. At the rare gatherings with other diggers, Lily heard exciting tales about the hunters' exploits. Rumour had it they did not always bring back all the food they found, even the precious meat.

"That means the hunters are breaking The Law!" Lily whispered to Maria.

"The hunters must sample their takings," Maria said, hiding a smile. "To make sure that the food is fit for the Authorities."

"I want to be a hunter."

"That is not your rank. You are a digger. The Authorities decided this for you when you were born."

"Why? And don't just say they obeyed The Law. Who made The Law anyway?"

"The Goddess made The Law and everything in our world."

Lily thought this over. Every digger knew the Goddess made the world, and that She had created the Authorities in her own image. Of course, no one had any idea what the

Goddess looked like, or the mechanism whereby She passed on Her word to The Authorities.

"What if the Goddess got it wrong?"

"Enough! No more questions."

Not understanding the reasons for what happened in the world made Lily feel stupid. She longed to go to school, but education of diggers was forbidden. Learning was reserved for the privileged. Maria reminded her yet again that their low status was an advantage. To be overlooked meant to be safe.

"Are hunters allowed to learn?" Lily persisted.

"Only enough to navigate the Outer World, so they can bring food home to our citadel."

Now, more than ever, Lily wanted to become a hunter.

***

Lucy fidgeted on her kitchen chair. Every day Mom made peanut butter sandwiches for lunch, to save money, so Dad could have steak for dinner. To keep his strength up, Mom said. Because he was the one who travelled to earn money for the family.

"Time for your lessons, dear." Miriam gathered up their dirty dishes, clearing the way for Lucy's textbooks.

"Why do I have to learn at home? Why can't I go to school like other children? And don't just say it's God's will."

Miriam sighed. Lucy was always so full of questions. "Your father and I decided to home-school you the day you came into our lives. Public schools don't follow God's word, so the children there just learn about sex and drugs. I know you're lonely, but out here we're safe. And you'll stay pure."

***

The Outer World where the hunters searched for food remained a tantalizing mystery for Lily. She knew it only as a breath of fresh air gusting through a tunnel or a beckoning light at the end of a long passageway. She yearned to see it for herself.

"You would not like it," Maria said, in response to her pestering. "The Outer World is full of perils. Most hunters eventually die there. And they die horribly. At least as diggers we are protected inside the Citadel."

Except for the constant landslides and falling rocks in the tunnels, Lily thought. And the earthquakes and floods, cataclysms launched from the Outer World without rhyme or reason. One very old digger claimed that long ago a meteor pulverized the citadel, resulting in a huge loss of life. Rebuilding their home had taken her entire lifetime.

If I were a hunter, I would not suffocate in the tunnels the next time a meteor hits, Lily thought.

She bided her time until she and Maria reached their most remote working site. Maria had always forbidden her to venture into the tunnel with the glowing, faraway circle of light; she alone cleared that area. Lily's duty was to watch for the inspection guards. But Maria was older now and, often as not, Lily would spot her taking a snooze at the far end. This time, when she heard the soft whistling of Maria's snores, she ran into the tunnel, stepped over her sleeping form and looked out through the opening.

The light almost blinded her, but a stream of pure, dust-free air rushed through her body. Her energy surged, despite her nagging hunger. And as her eyes adjusted, the Outer World appeared in a bewildering array of colors. All her life, she had known only shades of black and brown, so she had no names for these.

She gazed down the earthen wall of the citadel. So this was how their home appeared to the Outer World! The slope looked steep, but negotiable for someone as young and agile as Lily.

Maria stirred beside her. She did not berate her, only gazed at her in sad silence. "I tried to protect you. Now it is too late."

"You never told me how beautiful the Outer World is," Lily said, drinking it in. "What is that color?" She pointed down at the flat plain that stretched to the horizon.

"That is green, the color of grass." And when Lily pointed upward. "That is the sky. Its color is called 'blue'."

"In the grass I see thousands of colored spots. Some are blue like the sky, but what are the names of the others? And the scents – this is what heaven, the home of the Goddess, must be like."

"Perhaps. The grass is our hunting ground. Those spots you see are called flowers. Some of them give us food."

"Oh, why did the Authorities not make me a hunter? Why do they want me to suffer?"

"To suffer is our lot in life as diggers," Maria said wearily. "Now come away from the lookout. Remember The Law."

***

The air felt so humid and still, real thunderstorm weather. Miriam spotted Lucy by the kitchen door. In her hand, the girl held her father's rusty old tool box, the one she called her explorer kit.

"You'll have to stay inside this afternoon, dear."

While her daughter sulked in front of the television, Miriam took the remote and switched to the weather channel. A tornado warning for their area popped up on the screen.

"I want to play outside. I want to go to the end of fields," Lucy said.

"I don't like you wandering off where I can't see you. And, believe me, there's nothing to see out there. Just more fields that look exactly like the one behind our garden."

"That's not true. I want to find the blown-down house."

Miriam's glance drifted to the kitchen window. She silently cursed their landlord, the old farmer, for filling Lucy's head with lurid stories. Especially the one about the tornado hitting the neighbours' farmhouse, killing the mother and her baby.

She shivered. Their house didn't have a tornado shelter or even a basement. But God wouldn't send another twister here, would He? He wouldn't take another family. He couldn't be that cruel.

She closed her eyes and reminded herself to have faith.

***

Returning to the lookout became as essential to Lily as breathing. She coaxed and pleaded with Maria to work in the remote passage.

The sky was not always blue during their visits. Sometimes it had glorious tones of red and pink – and the large golden circle that Maria called "the sun" did not burn her eyes. Other times, though, dull grey clouds shrouded its beauty and torrents of water poured down from above, thundering against the walls of the citadel.

"That is rain," Maria told her.

Lily had always associated water with floods and death, but in the Outer World, it meant life. The flowers smelled sweeter after the rain, and the grass of the plains glowed a deeper and lovelier green.

"How far do the plains reach?" she asked. "What lies beyond them?"

"No one knows," Maria replied. "Twice in my lifetime, the Authorities have dispatched the bravest and strongest of our hunters to explore the far reaches of the plains, but only a few returned. We cannot afford to waste precious resources on mere curiosity."

"But the hunters who returned, what did they find?"

Maria looked thoughtful. "Wondrous things. Strange flowers and beasts, caches of food, sometimes in huge abundance. Even other citadels, such as ours."

"Where? Where are these other citadels?"

"Far away at the end of the plains. Citadels can only exist where the soil is dry and the flowers edible. But even where conditions are perfect, there is no guarantee you will find intelligent life out there."

"Tell me about the beings in the other citadels. Do they look like us? Do they speak our language? Do they obey The Law?"

"My understanding is that all citadels in the world are organized much like ours. In some, I hear The Law is much harsher."

"Or perhaps their Law allows diggers to be free."

Maria's shrewd eyes took her in. "Don't even think about running away."

"What if I am? Perhaps in another citadel I could be a hunter."

"Get that ridiculous fairy tale out of your head! Even if you survived the plains and found another citadel, you would always be a foreigner there. And, if you're unlucky, the other beings will tear you to pieces simply because your color is different from theirs. I saw this happen with my own eyes."

Lily knew Maria never lied to her. "Were you... were you one of the explorer hunters?"

"Yes, long ago. I returned badly wounded and could no longer search for food. The Authorities wanted to retire me, but the Supreme Ruler spared my life. So now I continue to serve our citadel, but as a lowly digger."

Lily had a chilling thought. "What happens when you get too old to be a digger?"

"I will be retired. That is the Law."

***

Clouds covered the sky. A few raindrops pattered into the dry earth of the garden. Miriam gave up on the weather channel and turned on the radio. She strained to hear the local weather report over the blare of Lucy's television show.

Frustrated, she marched back into the living room and turned off the TV.

"Mom, you said I could watch it!" Lucy protested. "It's *Cosmos*, my favorite show. Dr. Tyson is talking about life on other planets."

"Your father doesn't like you watching TV. Especially that science show. God made the world. Science just explains His rules."

"Well, if God made the world, why did He make it so hot? Why does he make tornados? Why did he let that family get killed?"

"Because it's His will. Be quiet now." She picked up the telephone receiver and called the old farmer.

"Don't look too bad," he said in reply to her worries about the tornado warning. "But you're welcome to use our storm shelter. Drive yourselves on over." The kitchen door slammed behind her. She turned to see Lucy race outside with her explorer kit and disappear into the field behind the garden.

***

Lily dreaded the thought of Maria growing old. Though Maria could still shift her share of dirt and debris, she tired easily and her secret naps lasted much longer.

I will run away and take Maria with me, Lily thought. She was an explorer hunter. She will find us a friendly citadel. We have to escape, or we'll die as slaves.

She longed for the Outer World with an intensity that frightened her. She waited until Maria crept into a side tunnel for one of her lengthy naps, then raced back through the maze of passages to her beloved lookout.

I'll never have another chance, she thought, and leapt outside into the brightness.

She slid and tumbled down the sloping earth wall of the citadel to the edge of the flowers. Gathering her courage, she wandered into the grass, reveling in the splendor of the plains and the intoxicating colors and scents of the flowers. From time to time she spotted strange beasts among the plants, some larger, others smaller than she. None spoke her language. They uttered only strange clicks, buzzes or roars.

Suddenly she heard the tread of footsteps: a troop of hunters on the march. She hid in the tall grasses until they passed out of sight.

She had dallied too long. The light was fading. Inky black clouds were streaming over the beautiful blue of the sky.

Halfway up the sloping wall of the citadel, the rain hit, a bombardment of water that sent rivers snaking through the dirt. She scrambled for footing as the soil beneath her melted into lethal mud. Using the last of her strength, she hauled herself back into the safety of the lookout.

Maria was waiting for her. "All your life I have tried to protect you," she cried. "Don't you understand anything I have told you? When the guards discover what you've been up to, the Authorities will summon you to The Centre."

"I was careful. Nobody saw me."

"You think of no one but yourself. You are throwing your life away — and mine as well."

"I would never do anything to hurt you. And the Outer World isn't full of horror. All I found was beauty. None of the beasts there did me any harm."

"You were simply lucky."

"I felt far safer in the Outer World than I do here in the Citadel. Let's run away together. So what if we die? We'll die as free beings."

"Don't romanticize death. Look at yourself — the rains nearly finished you off. Was that so wonderful and full of beauty?"

"At least when the next meteor strikes, I won't be buried alive in rubble."

"You think so? A meteor can strike you down in the Outer World just as easily. And that is nothing compared to a comet, a pillar of fire that burns you alive."

"Another fairy tale!"

"A comet nearly killed me. Unbearable heat and light crashed down from the sky and struck our hunting troop. I watched my friends burn and shrivel into charred husks. I only escaped because I'd fallen behind them. All I could do was pray to the Goddess to save them."

"And She did nothing, of course." In the face of Maria's horrified expression, Lily went on, "I think The Authorities just made up The Law so they get to eat all the good food. They say there's a Goddess so we'll do what we're told."

"Then how do you explain the sun and the rain? Who made the plains, the beasts and the flowers, if not the Goddess? Who made us?"

"How can I answer that, when I'm not allowed to go to school? Believe in the Goddess if you like. I don't! The Goddess is just a fairy tale."

"Heresy!" cried a voice behind them. The deep, implacable voice of a guard.

In a heartbeat, they were surrounded and placed under arrest.

***

The weather had turned strange. Dark clouds loomed on the horizon, while the sun beat down hotter than ever. In the distance, Miriam heard the ominous rumble of thunder. She fiddled with the controls on the radio, searching for a signal. Suddenly all the lights went out.

She tried to phone the old farmer again, but heard only static on the line.

"Lucy!" Where had the girl gone?

Miriam grabbed her car keys and ran outside. Clouds were streaming across the sky. The first splats of rain hit her skin.

***

The guards dragged Lily and Maria down into the depths of citadel. The air grew ever more hot and stifling.

"I'm sorry," Lily told Maria, only to be silenced roughly by a guard. *I should have let myself be drowned in the rain,* she thought. *I would have died free, and Maria would be safe.*

She looked desperately up and down the passages, but saw no chance of escape. Other diggers scuttled away in fear. Maria trudged ahead of her, head bowed. Fear ate through her belly like acid.

The tunnels grew wider. They had reached the heart of the citadel.

The Hall of the Authorities stretched before them, an enormous cavern stacked with food and trophies from the Outer World. Bodies of diggers and children lined the walls.

"Attention!" cried one of the guards. "Bow down! Show your respect to the Authorities and the Supreme Ruler."

20 or more figures strolled into the hall, glossy from meat and a life without labor. They surrounded an enormous being, larger than any digger, hunter or guard Lily had ever seen.

"The Supreme Ruler will do you herself," said the guard beside her. "Hope she's quick about it for once. I'm starving."

So the stories about the missing children were true!

A clamor of shouts and screams echoed down the tunnels. Lily's first thought was the other diggers had come to witness their execution. In the next instant, a noise beyond all description crashed down the roof of the cavern and she was drowning in earth. All around her she heard muffled cries of "Meteor!"

She struggled, battling a flood of soil and rocks, calling for Maria. Ahead she saw light. Using her youthful strength and every skill she had learned as a digger, she fought her way toward it. Miraculously, she surfaced into the Outer World.

She didn't hesitate. She dashed into the grass of the plain heedless of the water left by the rain storm. A huge force crashed past her, knocking her down: the Supreme Ruler in full flight in a crowd of guards, hunters and diggers.

Lily took refuge in the flowers, hiding the same way she had eluded the hunters. A giant beam of light streaked down from the sky.

"Comet!" shrieked a fleeing digger.

The comet struck down the Supreme Ruler in midflight. She writhed in agony. Her limbs began to shrivel and, as Lily gazed on in horror, fire burst from her abdomen and consumed her.

Lily crouched in terror, watching the deadly comet strike down again and again, burning the fleeing inhabitants of the citadel.

Abruptly as it had appeared, the comet vanished. More meteors crashed down from the sky, crushing everything beneath them.

She prayed to the Goddess to stop the mad carnage.

"Don't punish the others. I was the one who broke The Law. Please don't let them die. Please save my mother."

Finally the meteors ceased. Rain began to fall, but Lily no longer cared. She wandered through the grasses, calling for Maria.

"Lily?" It was Maria's voice. She was limping toward her through the weeds, wounded but alive.

"Mother!" Lily rushed over to her. "You're safe! Thank the Goddess!"

"Yes, She looks after Her children. After all, She made us."

Together they made their way into the safety of the plains.

***

"Lucy!"

Frantic now, Miriam searched through the field. Lucy wouldn't have searched out that ruined house on her own, would she?

Overhead, the winds were making a strange pattern, blowing across each other. "Oh, God, please help me!" she prayed.

There! A few feet to her right, she spotted a faint trail of smoke.

"Lucinda!" She rushed over and snatched the magnifying glass from her daughter's hand. "How many times have I told you? You could start a brush fire and kill us all!"

Lucy glared at her. Her jeans and runners were coated with dirt from kicking over the large ant hill beside her.

"What you are doing is cruel! Ants are God's creatures. They have a right to live, too."

"They're just bugs."

Lucy could be so mean sometimes, so eager to hurt things smaller than she was. We know so little about her birth parents, Miriam thought. What if it's bad blood coming to the surface?

She grabbed Lucy's hand and pulled her back toward the house.

"My explorer kit! You forgot my explorer kit."

"Leave it!"

The winds hit them full force when they reached the deck. Miriam dragged Lucy over to the car which sat parked in front of the house.

She heaved Lucy into the passenger seat. The wind tore at her clothes as she struggled to climb in behind the steering wheel. She started the engine and pulled onto the highway, heading for the old farmer's place ten miles down the road.

"We must pray now, Lucy. Pray to God to save us."

Lucy's pale face stared at her. "Is that a tornado, Mom?"

Behind them, to the west, an ominous funnel cloud was taking shape. Miriam pressed the accelerator to the floor, praying her car would go faster.

"Don't worry, Lucy. God will save us. He looks after His children. After all, He made us."

AMDUR'S CAT

This light-hearted story is one of my personal favorites. I had great fun writing it. Tiddles was one of our beloved cats and he lives again in this story. Some of the antics at the Ministry of Health were inspired by a certain notorious Toronto mayor.

Published in Thirteen, An Anthology of Crime Stories *by the Mesdames of Mayhem, Carrick Publishing, 2013.*

On a snowy December night Benjamin Amdur saw a lion. It was gamboling about like a kitten swatting at the fat, wet snowflakes that tumbled through the dark. Right in the centre of Riverdale Park by the children's wading pool.

Under the lamps of the park's snowy pathway, the lion's tawny fur glowed like the back of an old velvet sofa. For a brief moment — that gap between the surreal world and biting reality – he watched as Rousseau's painted lion came to life.

Then he remembered the sleeping gypsy – the minstrel who was about to eaten.

He grasped the icy black iron fence beside him. The house it surrounded lay dark. At two in the morning, its inhabitants, like most normal people, were in bed. By the time he woke them up screaming for help, the lion would have torn out his throat.

With infinite caution, his eyes on the animal, he edged back into the shadows of Winchester Street, the road he'd weaved down moments before. Behind him, three blocks away, lay Parliament Street with its strip bars, eateries and mini-marts. Surely to God one of those places had to be open!

The lion leapt in the air. It snapped at the snowflakes as they fell. He heard the crunch of its jaws, saw the flash of its teeth. Its tail lashed back and forth.

Then it paused, raised its huge head and sniffed the air. Its nostrils twitched.

He saw me!

Amdur turned and ran like a mad man.

Adrenalin buoyed him up for the first few feet but deserted him almost immediately. He was 48 and 20 pounds overweight. His regular habit of walking to work did nothing to bolster his panic-stricken need to run. He tore down the slushy sidewalk, his mind fixed on the zebras of the veldt. Zebras that ran far more swiftly than he. Zebras brought down and eviscerated alive...

By the time he reached the yellow lights of Parliament Street his chest was heaving. He doubled over, gasping for oxygen. If the lion got him now, he was dinner. But he couldn't take another step.

He looked frantically up and down the street. Every storefront was dark.

No buses, no taxis, no cars.

Then he spotted an angel standing under a streetlight a few yards to the south. Well, not an angel exactly, but a young police officer, her uniform immaculate, the brim of her cap spotless, her leather boots and gun holster gleaming with polish.

He summoned his remaining strength and stumbled over to her. "Oh, thank God...an animal...danger..." He couldn't stop panting. "Very dangerous. Over by ...Riverdale Farm."

She raised a tidy eyebrow. "Are you quite all right, sir?"

"No...no, I'm not all right." With the dispassion of his medical training, he estimated his heart to be thumping at 180 beats per minute. His blood pressure didn't bear thinking about. "You...help...must get help."

"How much have you had to drink tonight, sir?"

"Drink?" he echoed.

"Quite a few, I'd say. Identification, please."

"What?" Finally he caught his breath. "Please, you don't understand. There's a bloody great animal running around loose. It'll rip someone apart. We have to stop it."

"Your ID. Now!" Her hand moved toward her baton.

Amdur dragged out his wallet and handed her his driver's license. Her laser stare burned through its laminate cover.

"Dr. Benjamin Amdur." She studied his face with more than an element of disbelief. "So you're a doctor."

"Yes, I'm with the Ministry of Health. I'm Assistant Deputy Minister in charge of OHIP."

That made no impression on her whatsoever. "OHIP?"

"Your, I mean, *our* free medicine in Ontario. Look here, we're wasting time."

"How many drinks have you had tonight, sir?"

"What the hell does it matter? I was at a Christmas party, for heaven's sake. At the National Club." That lofty name made even less impression on her. "I tell you I know what I saw. There's a lion on the loose."

"Lion! Why didn't you say so!"

"I did say so."

"Where? Where did you see it?"

"In Riverdale Park, by the children's wading pool...the farm."

She shoved his license in her tunic and tore down Winchester Street, leaving him standing there like an idiot. He chased after her, but she set a blistering pace. He only managed to catch up with her at the edge of the park.

No sign of the lion.

Amdur squinted through the heavy curtain of falling snow. Where was the beast? Where was it? The grounds of the park stretched out before him, white and featureless under the thick drifts.

"I don't see any lion." The police officer scanned the area with her hard dark eyes. "Show me exactly where you saw him."

"Right over there!" Amdur pointed to the spot.

"OK, let's go. You first."

"I don't think that's wise."

"I'll be the judge of that." She unbuttoned her holster. "Get going or I'll arrest you. For wasting police time."

"Fine, fine."

The pathway lay buried in snow. He trudged through the heavy wet drifts toward the dark shapes of Riverdale Farm, a miserable King Wenceslas with his testy page behind him.

By the time they arrived at the snowed-in wading pool, he was thoroughly chilled. "The lion was here." He scanned the ground for paw prints but saw nothing. "He was running around right here, I swear it. The snow must have covered his tracks."

"Right, sure. One side." She pushed past him, bending down to study the snow drift in front of them. Suddenly she stiffened. "Did you hear that?"

"No, nothing." The falling snow muffled all sound.

"Over there." She pointed to a tangled clump of bushes a few feet away, stood up and unbuttoned her gun holster. "Stay here." She headed for the bushes.

"Wait! For heaven's sake, call for back-up."

She vanished behind the twisted mass of branches. The lion must be behind it, lurking…

Amdur fumbled for his Blackberry. Why had he trusted that inexperienced young constable? She was going to get them both killed.

He tried to punch out 911, but the phone slithered from his frozen hands and plopped into the snow. He kneeled down and foraged desperately for it. By the time his numb fingers retrieved it, he was staring at the police officer's polished boots.

He stumbled to his feet. "You're back. You're all right."

"Score ten out of ten, Captain Obvious. You can put your phone away now."

"Where's the lion? Did you see him?"

"Oh, yeah, right. The lion. Sure, I saw him. Teeth like a raptor. I've got him right here."

He noticed belatedly that she was clutching a furry wet bag in her arms. The bag came to life with a piercing cry.

"Here take him."

Before he had a chance to react, she heaved the soaking bundle at him. It thudded against his chest. Long, curved claws dug into his cashmere overcoat.

"That's a cat!"

"No kidding."

"I didn't see a cat. I saw a lion!"

"Right, sure you did. Time to go home. You first." She pointed the way out of the park.

"This isn't my cat. I don't own a cat." He tried in vain to detach the animal's claws. "Look, I can't just take him."

"Fine, doctor." The word 'doctor' rang with the respect she no doubt reserved for pimps and pederasts. "Here's your choice. Either you take your cat home all nice and quiet or I throw you in the drunk tank. How about that? I bet that'd go down real well with your fancy-ass friends at the National Club."

"For God's sake!" He gripped the cat with his free hand and shoved his phone back into his coat pocket with the other. He felt exhausted — and admittedly too well-oiled — to argue any further.

She'd read his address from the front of his driver's license, so she knew exactly where he lived. He stumbled out of the park to Sumach Street, then north to the tall brick Victorian house that held his flat. Both she and the cat stuck with him up to the front door.

"Keys!" She held out a gloved hand.

Swearing, he clutched the cat with one chilled hand, dug out his keys with the other and handed them over.

Once safe inside his flat, he tried to detach the cat, but it let out a terrifying howl.

"Damn it, the cat will wake the other tenants. What do I do?"

She laughed and tossed his keys down on the hardwood floor next to his soaking feet. "Dry him off and feed him. Give him tuna. Cats like tuna."

"And what the hell do I do about his other end?"

"Tear up some newspaper. Throw it in a box. And don't forget, Dr. Amdur. I know where you live." She snapped the edge of his driver's license and flipped it down onto the floor next to his keys.

With that, she slammed his front door shut and left.

And he'd taken her for an angel! She was a demon, a witch — and this wretched lump of wetness attached to his chest was her familiar.

He lurched down the hall to the bathroom, the cat clinging to his overcoat like grim death. He yanked a bath towel off the heated rack, wrapped it around the animal and tried to dry it off. It shuddered with cold and meowed piteously. After a few more minutes of rubbing, it looked slightly less than a demonic imp from hell. He could see that although its fur was mostly black, it had white paws like socks. A red leather collar circled its neck. It had to be someone's pet.

"There you go, cat." At long last, he managed to extract its claws from his coat. He set it down on the tiles next to the radiator. Now he had to feed the damn thing.

He made his way to the kitchen. On his way there, he flung off his sodden coat and retrieved his keys and driver's license. *I'm going mad*, he thought, shivering. *Hallucinating. Seeing lions of all things.*

He seized the bottle of cognac standing on the granite counter, poured himself a generous shot and downed it.

Alzheimer's at 48, he thought. Rare, but medically possible. *Or maybe it's because the wretched Tories got elected by a landslide – that's what's pushed me over the edge.*

He faced an unpleasant Executive Committee meeting first thing in the morning. The Assistant Deputy Ministers' formal introduction to the new Minister of Health, a man named Herb Cott, a first-time MPP and an as yet unknown quantity. Amdur's IT staff had scoured the internet and uncovered that Cott's life experience was limited to running a bait shop. In the same riding where the new Premier kept his family cottage, of course.

From selling worms to managing the multi-billion dollar operations of the Ministry of Health. Wonderful! Amdur poured himself another shot of cognac.

"Meow!" The cat had followed him into the kitchen. It crouched on the slate tiles, its luminous green eyes looking up at him expectantly.

Right, feed the damn cat. He set down his empty glass and searched through the cupboards. No tuna, but he did have some canned salmon. It was Nora, his wife's favorite comfort food. Even now with Nora gone, he couldn't resist buying it whenever he made the effort to go grocery shopping.

He opened the can, slopped a few spoonfuls onto a saucer and set it down on the floor. The cat gave it a tentative sniff.

"Salmon not good enough for you?" Amdur opened his stainless steel refrigerator and found a carton of milk. He poured a little milk into a soup bowl and turned to give it to the cat. The salmon had disappeared.

"That was fast work." He set the milk down in front of the cat, fetched a dry bath towel from the bathroom, folded it and put it down in front of the kitchen radiator.

"There's your spot," he told it.

Now for the other end. He glanced at his watch. Already time for the morning paper to be delivered. Given its praise for the Tories' promised deep cuts to health care spending, he couldn't think of a better use for it.

But when he opened the outside door to pick up the paper, he noticed a large shopping bag sitting on the verandah. Inside it he found a plastic litter pan, kitty litter and several cans of cat food.

And a handwritten note that said, *I know where you live.*

***

He woke with a start three hours later. The cat had crawled onto the foot of his bed while he slept. It purred as he examined the red leather collar around its neck. No tags, nothing that could identify its owner.

"What am I going to do with you?" he said to the cat as he got ready for work. "No time to find your owner this morning. I'm already fiendishly late."

Despite grabbing a taxi, he was the last of the ADM's to arrive at the Executive Committee Boardroom. Vladimir Nickle, the aged Deputy Minister, raised a sparse eyebrow in disapproval. Amdur's colleagues shouted their ribald greetings, ignoring Nickle as usual. Nickle's lengthy and ineffectual sojourn at the Ministry had allowed them to run their divisions as they pleased – and assured their ongoing loyalty to him.

Amdur tossed out a few cheerful zingers in reply before he dropped into his usual chair beside his friend and ally, Judy Reed, the ADM of Communications and Community Health. A blissful aroma of fresh coffee emanated from the credenza over by the wall, reminding him that he'd missed breakfast. He noticed that Nickle had dusted off the Ministry's official china set and even ordered muffins in honour of Cott's visit.

"Muffins!" Amdur eyed them hungrily. "Nickle never budgets for food. Even at Christmas," he whispered to Judy.

"Cott won't care about Nickle's little party," she whispered back. "My sources tell me the Premier's staff call him The Cutter. He hates all forms of government. In fact, he calls us bureaucrats 'civil serpents'."

"What did we poor overworked government buggers do to him? Turn down his fishing license?"

"Don't joke. The Cutter's catchphrase is: I'm derailing the government gravy train."

"Hardly auspicious."

Amdur glanced at his watch. Minister Cutter and his retinue were already several minutes late. Casual conversations broke out around the table. Nickle appeared to be dozing off.

Since Judy ran a cat rescue service during her meager spare time, Amdur entertained her with the tale of his late night adventures — though he carefully omitted any mention of the lion.

"The way that police officer behaved!" she said. "That poor kitty! His owners must be frantic. You should file a complaint with Toronto Police Services."

"Oh, I can't be bothered. I'll drop the cat off at the Humane Society tonight."

"Well, you could do that, I suppose. But many owners don't think to look there for their lost pets. I know a faster way. Is the cat chipped?"

"You mean a microchip?"

"Yes, vets sometimes put a chip under the cat's skin. It holds the owner's contact information. I know a nice vet in Riverdale. Why don't you take the cat there? Ask him to read your cat's chip."

"Fine, but how do I carry the bloody cat over to the vet clinic? I need a leash or something."

Judy laughed. "I have a spare cat carrier in my office. Drop by and pick it up." She laid a warning hand on his arm. "Heads up."

Nickle's eyes had creaked open. He uttered a dry cough. "Gentlemen, ladies. Time is rather getting on. Have any of you had word...from your respective staffs...that perhaps..."

"Our new guy is wandering around doing an impromptu inspection?" one of the other ADM's filled in.

"Exactly."

A flurry of Blackberries and iPads hit the table. After a lot of furious tapping and hushed conversations, everyone came up empty. No sign of the new minister.

Nickle heaved a windy sigh. "Rather a basic question perhaps, but do we know what our new Minister looks like? He is ...um...rather an unknown quantity. Do we perchance have a...um...photograph?"

Glances were exchanged. Amdur pulled up a file on his iPad, quietly blessing his IT staff for covering his backside. "This is him."

He passed his iPad to Nickle who passed it on. It circled the boardroom table to cries of "He's fishing in his canoe, how cute." "People voted for that?" "Who's uglier, him or the pickerel he just caught?"

"Might I have your attention?" Nickle's voice sounded surprisingly strong. "Benjamin, you're the practical one. Would you mind..."

"Of course." Amdur rose and left the boardroom, taking his iPad with him.

Rather than searching aimlessly through the rabbit warren of corridors at Queen's Park, he took the elevator straight down the main lobby. To his relief one of the senior security guards, Ludmilla, an uncompromising Russian immigrant, sat on duty at the main reception desk.

"Sure, I see this weirdo." She handed him back his iPad. "He say, hey you lady, take me to Minister's office. So I say, sure, no problem, but Minister he is busy guy. You go down hall to Service Ontario. Stand in line for your health card like normal peoples."

Disaster, Amdur thought. He rushed down the hall to the Service Ontario office, looking frantically for signs of the Minister's party. In the crowded room, he spotted no well-tailored people who could be Cott or his aides.

He handed his iPad to the receptionist sitting at the entrance to Service Ontario. She studied the screen and pointed to the waiting area. There in the front row, his back to them, sat a rumpled fiftyish man, alone.

Amdur straightened his posture and walked over to him. It was Cott all right, a scowl on his face and a number slip in his hand.

"Minister Cott?"

Bloodshot eyes stared up at him from under a set of shaggy brows. Cott wore a hunting vest over his red plaid shirt. His stained khaki pants were shoved into a pair of muddy rubber boots. No hat graced his close-cropped head.

"We're waiting for you upstairs, Minister. Is your team with you?"

"Nope."

Cott heaved his bulk out of the chair and followed Amdur out of the Service Ontario office. When they passed security in the main lobby, Cott balled up the paper number and tossed it in Ludmilla's face.

Amdur cleared his throat in protest, but Cott had already barreled over to the elevators. They continued their journey upstairs in deathly silence.

When they reached the top floor, Amdur ushered Cott down the hall into the Executive Boardroom. None of the ADM's could conceal their surprise. The pickerel had landed.

Nickle creaked to his feet and offered Cott his chair. Cott plunked himself down and said nothing. He made a slow study of each of the ADM's in turn.

A staring contest, Amdur realized, annoyed at Cott's childish power game. He watched Nickle teeter over to the credenza, pour out a cup of coffee and shakily set it down in front of the new Minister.

Cott looked at it. "What's that? You trying to poison me?"

Nickle uttered a dry laugh. "Good joke, Minister. Very good joke." He signaled to the others to join in the laughter. No one did.

"Go sit over there." Cott pointed Nickle to the chairs along the side of the room where his aides, had they been there, were supposed to sit. Nickle shrugged and did as he was told.

Cott leaned his burly forearms on the boardroom table. "Now then. Your Ministry eats up 30 billion of dollars every single year. Your Ministry eats up more'n any other goddamn government department. Hell, it eats up more'n all them departments combined. That's money you guys steal right out of the taxpayer's wallet."

"With respect, Minister, Ontario taxpayers do get considerable benefits from our health care system," Amdur put in.

"Oh, you think so, eh? I'll tell you what the taxpayers want. They want choice. They don't want no nanny state. They want their freedom back."

"You mean freedom to die if you can't afford a doctor or a hospital," Judy said from her place next to Amdur.

Cott ignored her. "Now you all listen up good. No more swimming around in gravy. I'm cutting your health budget by 50 percent. That's right: 50 percent. That's what I told the voters I'd do when I got elected and you're gonna watch me do it. Next year, I'm cutting you buggers back another 50 percent. You wanna keep working here, you'll do what I say. Understand?"

In the stunned silence that followed, Cott foraged in his hunting vest for a cigar. He leaned back, clumped his muddy feet on the mahogany table and lit up.

"Minister, the…um…presentations," Nickle ventured from his exile next to the muffins .

"Save it. I'm gonna meet with each and every one of you." Cott pointed with his cigar. "And each of you is gonna have to prove to me why I don't just axe you and your whole damn department." He swayed forward, thumping his feet on the floor. "And in case any of you civil serpents get any ideas, remember: Herb Cott stabs from the front."

"No problem, Minister," Amdur couldn't help saying. "I believe you've come to the right place."

***

"You certainly didn't help matters," Judy said later that afternoon when Amdur dropped by her office to pick up the cat carrier.

"Sorry." Amdur slumped into the chair facing her desk. "The world's gone mad. A fool of a worm seller bent on destroying the health system of 14 million people."

"I know." She wiped her nose with a tissue.

"Good heavens, Judy. You've been crying."

"Close the door." While he did so, she opened the bottom drawer of her desk and pulled out a bottle of scotch and two glasses. "Join me?"

"Of course." He watched her pour out two generous shots. "What's happened?"

"Cott was just here. He accused me and my division of handing out freebies to illegal immigrants and perverts. He's closing down all the walk-in clinics in the province, starting with the AIDS clinics."

"That's illegal. He'll never get away with it."

"The Tories have a majority in the House. They can do whatever they like. The Cabinet will simply pass an executive order. They could do it tonight."

Amdur took a large swallow of scotch. Crazy as it sounded, Judy was right.

"It's not the money, Ben. Mother and I will manage somehow. But if Cott fires me or I quit my job, who will fight for the AIDS clinics? He's flushing 30 years of progress down the drain."

"We *all* have to fight Cott. All the ADM's together."

"We'll all be fighting too hard to protect our own turfs. You know how it works."

Maybe we're not civil serpents as much as rats, Amdur thought.

"Cott's a horrible, petty little man." Judy swiped at her nose. "He's cancelled all vacations until further notice. Everyone in the Ministry has to work through Christmas. If he fires you, he's making you work the mandatory two week notice period. And that includes Christmas, of course. Lay-offs start tomorrow. He bragged about it!"

"That bastard!" Amdur drained his glass. "No one takes my staff without a fight."

But he knew he was facing the fight of his life.

***

The cat was waiting by the front door when Amdur returned home that night. It purred loudly and rubbed itself against his legs.

"Well, cat, you're the only happy person I've seen today."

He made for the kitchen and heard it patter in after him. While he heated up a frozen dinner in the microwave, he opened one of the cans of cat food the police officer had left him.

"Disgusting muck." Amdur stared at the can's contents and refilled the cat's dish. "Like pate that's gone off. But you seem to like it well enough."

The cat made a strange humming noise while it ate, purring and chewing at the same time.

He poured out milk for the cat and a large glass of Bordeaux for himself. When his dinner was ready, he carried it into his study and set it down on the desk next to his laptop. With all the day's distractions, he faced hours of more work before bed.

I've got to put a stop to The Cutter, but how? he thought. *I can't even trust my own brain. Did I see that wretched lion or didn't I?*

He gulped down his meal while he combed the internet for reports of escaped lions in Toronto. Nothing. Frustrated, he pulled out his Blackberry and dialed Toronto Police Services. After an excruciating maze of telephone menus, he reached the duty officer.

"No sir, no reports about lions missing from the Toronto Zoo. Are you quite sure that's what you saw?"

Time to track down the cat-throwing police officer, Amdur decided. Filing a complaint would make him feel better.

He told the duty officer what had happened.

"Did she give you her name and badge number?"

"No, I forgot to ask."

"Sir, the force has over 5,000 sworn officers. And a lot of them are dark-haired females in their twenties."

"Surely to God you know the names of the officers on patrol in Riverdale last night!"

"Sure do. Constables Chan and Wong. Both male. Have yourself a nice night, sir."

Amdur was left listening to the dial tone. *Wonderful,* he thought. *Now the police have me down on their weirdo list.*

"Meow!" The cat appeared near his chair. In the next instant, it leapt onto his desk and knocked over his wine glass.

"Damn it, cat." He wiped up the wine. "Never mind. Time for me to get to work." The cat stretched out across his keyboard. "Enough foolishness." He lifted the cat onto his lap where it settled down. More purring.

It stayed put while Amdur quenched the critical issues burning in his division. At the same time, he tried to reassure his staff that the Ministry wasn't going down like the Titanic.

Ha, bloody ha, he thought.

At midnight an urgent e-mail appeared in his inbox. Nickle had resigned his post as deputy minister.

Amdur leaned back, absently stroking the cat. "Poor Nickle. What a cold-hearted Merry Christmas after 45 years of service! Inevitable, I suppose." He sighed. "Tell me, cat, what did you see last night? Did *you* see the lion?"

The cat looked up attentively. Its pointed black and white face was rather sweet, Amdur thought.

"I can't just keep calling you 'cat'. All right, while you're staying with me, why don't I call you Tiddles? That's the name of my wife, Nora's cat, the one she grew up with. He was quite the character apparently. I used to enjoy her stories about Tiddles. You see, I never had pets as a child. Too difficult in central London, especially with both parents working as doctors."

Amdur roused himself. It wouldn't do to get attached to the cat. It belonged with its owners, whoever they were.

He searched out the website of the vet clinic Judy had recommended. It opened early in the morning. He'd have just enough time to drop by with Tiddles before work.

***

The Saint Francis Animal Hospital sat on Parliament Street, a short distance down from Peepers, Riverdale's notorious strip club.

At least the strippers have some Christmas spirit, Amdur thought as he lugged the cat carrier past the club to the vet clinic. Red and green lights were ablaze in its garish marquee and massive Christmas wreaths adorned its tarnished brass doors.

He and Tiddles were the animal hospital's first customers. A tiny dark man in medical greens introduced himself as the veterinarian, Dr. Ali.

"Muhammad Ali, actually," the vet said as he showed them into the examination room. "This is a big joke, yes?"

Amdur tried to smile. He set the cat carrier down on the steel examining table and tried to extricate Tiddles. The cat had resisted getting into the carrier and now only a nuclear bomb could dislodge him.

"Allow me." Dr. Ali dug some cat treats out of his jacket pocket. They worked like magic. Tiddles emerged and in short order, allowed himself to be examined. "How long have you owned your kitty?"

Amdur explained that he'd found Tiddles in Riverdale Park.

"I see. Well, your lost kitty is a neutered male. Looking at his teeth, I would say he is about five years old." The vet ran his gentle hands down Tiddles' sides. "He is rather thin, but his coat is thick. I would agree with you, doctor, that he is somebody's pet. He has a lovely nature, but...he is nervous. Has he suffered a trauma?"

"A predator chased him. A li—." Amdur stopped himself just in time.

"Exactly! Coyotes and foxes travel down the ravine system to hunt in our city. The outdoors is dangerous for kitties." He fingered the scruff of Tiddles' neck. "Good news. The kitty has a chip. I will read it and try to locate his owner."

He picked up Tiddles and carried him through the connecting door of the examination room into the innards of the animal hospital.

Alone for the moment, Amdur called his executive assistant, Leslie Wong, on his Blackberry.

"So far no earth-shattering crises – or at least they can wait till you get here," she told him. "Oh, and Otto Winter, your IT security consultant, wants to see you."

Wonderful, Amdur thought. Otto never asked for a meeting unless his IT crisis *was* earth-shattering. "Very well. Tell Otto I'll see him for lunch at my usual pub." He couldn't afford the time to eat lunch, but now he couldn't afford not to.

He finished the call just as Dr. Ali returned with Tiddles.

"I have good news and bad news," the vet said. "The good news is that I have located the kitty's owner."

"And the bad news?"

"I have spoken with her. She lives in Mississauga."

"But how could Tiddles end up in Riverdale Park? He'd have to cross 30 kilometers of highways and busy city streets to get here."

"Exactly. Sad to say some cat owners are not good people. When they no longer want their kitty, they simply throw him away. In a park or a cemetery."

"I can't return Tiddles to that woman. She'll only dump him somewhere else."

"True enough. Luckily, she does not want him back. But she did say a strange thing. She claims he ran away in June. Obviously he has not been living rough for six months. He has found a new home in this area. This is the owner you must locate."

Amdur's heart sank. "What do you suggest?"

"My staff will put up a notice. That sometimes works. And you might call the other vet clinics near here."

Amdur thought hard for a moment. "Tell me, do you know of an animal hospital that deals with, um, much larger animals?"

"Do you mean horses? Or farm animals?"

"No, I meant…a lion."

"A lion?" Dr. Ali laughed, highly amused. "Heavens, no! To own such a beast in downtown Toronto would be highly illegal. Why do you ask?"

"Oh…er… curiosity." The ring of his Blackberry saved him from further explanation. He recognized Judy Reed's name on the call display. She sounded panic-stricken when he answered.

"I just stepped out to call you. Cott and his crew are in my office. They're coming to see you next. And, Ben, Cott is on the warpath."

***

No time to take Tiddles home. Amdur quickly paid the vet clinic and hailed a cab outside. While the taxi tore down Wellesley Street to Queen's Park, he phoned Leslie, his executive assistant, to warn her about Cott's imminent arrival.

"Take the freight elevator. I'll meet you," she said. "Judy will try to stall them another five minutes."

When he got to Queen's Park, Ludmilla, the security guard, unlocked the freight elevator for him and sent him and Tiddles up to his floor.

Leslie was waiting for him when he arrived. He tore off his overcoat and gloves and handed them to her. But when he tried to give her the cat carrier, she waved it away, eyes and nose streaming.

"I can't, Ben. Allergies…"

He could hear Cott's rough voice approaching. No time. He ran into his office, sat down behind his desk and shoved Tiddles' carrier beneath it.

"No noise, Tiddles." He had only seconds to fire up his iPad before Cott burst into his office with two men behind him.

The first, a tall bulky man, closed Amdur's door and took up position in front of it. Obviously a private bodyguard. The other much smaller, thinner man set down his briefcase and introduced himself as Cott's lawyer.

Both Cott's aides wore expensive suits. Perhaps that was why The Cutter had switched his hunting gear for a dusty blue blazer over a golf shirt. Muddy Doc Martins replaced his rubber boots. He sat down in the visitor's chair opposite Amdur's desk without asking. The lawyer stayed on his feet.

"You've gotta lot of computer types in your shop," Cott said without preamble. "You can tell 'em their jobs are going. Over to India where they do the same stuff for cheap."

"I regret, Minister, that simply won't be possible," Amdur said.

"What's your problem? Look at you. You're from there and you're working here."

"I'm a Canadian citizen via England." Amdur breathed deeply to stay calm. "And Minister, you cannot replace a Canadian's job with a foreign national. It's against the law."

"Corporations ship jobs offshore all the time. Hell, one of the big banks just did it."

"And got in a lot of trouble for it."

"So what? Get used to idea. And fast." Cott pulled out a cigar and pointed it at the lawyer. "You, fix it."

The lawyer coughed discreetly. "With all due respect, Minister. Dr. Amdur does have a point."

"He does, does he?" Cott lit up.

"Would you mind putting that out?" Amdur said. "My executive assistant is extremely allergic to tobacco smoke."

"She's not here."

"She will be in my office after you leave."

Cott scowled. The lawyer plucked the smoldering cigar from his fingers and walked it over to the security guard, who took it outside.

"Where's he going? I need my protection," Cott said.

"He'll only be gone a moment," the lawyer assured him. "In the meantime, we have that other more serious issue to discuss."

At that moment, Tiddles let out an unearthly howl from where he sat trapped in the cat carrier.

"What the hell was that?" Cott looked around frantically.

"Nothing." Amdur folded his hands on top of the desk. "Did you hear anything?" he asked the lawyer.

"Um...not sure. The issue, Minister?"

"Oh, yeah." Cott collected himself. "You got a criminal working for you. In security no less. Now *that's* gotta be illegal."

"Ah, you must mean Otto Winter," Amdur said "He's our security expert. And yes, he does have a suspended sentence for computer hacking. An old sentence, I'd like to point out. He's saved Ontario taxpayers tens of millions of dollars by tracking down health care fraud."

"So what? Fire him."

"I can't."

"Can't or won't?"

"Both. I refuse to fire an excellent member of my staff without cause. And may I point out, Minister, I'm sure you don't want a lawsuit for unfair dismissal on your hands."

Cott looked at his lawyer. "Can the Winter guy do that?"

"I'm afraid so, Minister," the lawyer said.

"Bull crap. He don't have the bucks to sue." Cott leaned forward, pointing. "Now you listen to me…"

Tiddles let out another anguished howl. Cott froze, index finger in midair. "You…you've got a cat in here. A cat!"

"I'm sure he doesn't, Minister." The lawyer threw a worried glance at Amdur. "You don't, do you?"

Busted, Amdur thought. "Actually, I do. Tiddles is our divisional house cat. I find that he's good for employee morale. And improved productivity."

"Protection…where's my protection?" Cott's pudgy features took on a strange purplish hue. "He's killing me…I can't breathe."

Amdur leaped up to intervene, worried that The Cutter had a bad heart, but the lawyer waved him off and helped Cott to his feet.

"Herb, it's OK. We're going, OK? And Amdur is going to get rid of the damn cat. Right?"

"As you wish."

Wheezing, Cott leaned on Amdur's desk. "You…you planned this. You tried to kill me. You're dead…you hear me? You're dead."

He shook off his lawyer's helping hand and stumbled out of Amdur's office. The lawyer shrugged, picked up his briefcase and followed him.

Amdur sank back into his chair. "Well, Tiddles, I believe we've witnessed the worst case of felinophobia I've ever seen. And now since I've been declared dead, I am going to lunch."

***

A biting wind tore down Bay Street, chilling Amdur as he walked south with Tiddles to his favorite pub, The Duke of Somerset. The hostess smiled when she recognized him and turned a blind eye to the cat carrier. She led him to his usual booth at the back where a fat sixtyish man sat nursing a glass of foamy beer.

Amdur slid into the booth opposite Otto Winter. He put the cat carrier on the bench, its mesh gate facing him so he could keep an eye on Tiddles.

"New friend, doctor? Personally I prefer the ladies." Otto grinned over his beer. His cropped grey hair and stubbly jowls reminded Amdur of a decayed storm trooper.

"Never mind the cat. What's the problem?"

"Better get your beer first. You will need it." Otto groped through his grubby back pack and heaved a battered laptop onto the table.

Amdur ordered a much-needed pint of Boddingtons ale. It arrived in a flash and he took a grateful swallow. "All right, how bad is the bad news?"

"Our new dictator, Cott the Cutter, tried to hack into your email. Indeed he tried to explore the confidential files of your entire division."

"What!"

"Not to worry. No one gets through my firewalls. But Cott certainly has been a busy little beaver."

"But Cott's an idiot worm salesman. He can't be doing the hacking himself."

"Of course not. His lawyer hired a computer rat in Asia to do Cott's dirty work. A sneaky little rat, but sadly for him, not a deep thinker. I amused myself a little then boom! I spiked him. For me, a piece of delicious cake." Otto finished his beer and fished a rumpled envelope from the pocket of his equally rumpled jacket. "My resignation."

"Over my dead body!" Amdur banged down his beer glass. "The Ministry needs you. Now more than ever."

Otto shrugged his heavy shoulders. "You may change your mind in a minute. You see, last night after I fixed the rat, I made a wormhole in Cott's firewall. And up periscope!" He twisted his index finger to demonstrate.

"I shouldn't be hearing this."

"Even your cat could breach Cott's el-cheapo security. Relax, Doctor. No one detected my ghost in The Cutter's infernal machine." Otto laced his fingers over his ample paunch. "Now ask me anything."

"Otto, I'm going to pretend this conversation never happened."

"I knew you would have scruples. Too bad." Otto nudged his resignation letter over to Amdur's side of the table. "Cott spends all his time on line watching porno."

"How depressingly predictable!"

"Allow me to share the kinky details over lunch. My parting gift to the Ministry."

Otto fired up his laptop.

***

Otto's resignation letter in his pocket, Amdur flagged down a cab after lunch and took Tiddles home. While the taxi waited outside, he released the cat from his carrier and refilled his dishes. *Poor Tiddles,* he thought as he gave him a pat, *you've had a tough day. But then again, haven't we all?*

The darkening skies matched his mood as the cab returned him to Queen's Park. Ludmilla barely acknowledged him when he passed by the reception desk. No doubt after her run-in with Cott, she was working her two week notice through Christmas.

Back on his floor, he found Leslie stripping the ornaments off the office Christmas tree.

"Cott just cancelled all staff Christmas parties," she said. "All decorations are to be taken down. Not work-related he says, that SOB."

"Leave the tree up. Put the decorations back on. I'll deal with Cott and his boys personally if they bother us about it."

"Thanks, Ben. I could use some Christmas cheer right now."

"And we're throwing a farewell party for Nickle tomorrow morning. Here in my office. Call the caterers, send me the bill. Invite the whole damn Ministry."

"I'll get right on it. And never mind the caterers. We all do potluck at Christmas."

I've got to neutralize Cott, but how? Amdur thought. For the rest of the day he tried to focus on work, but his mind teemed with the unwanted images of Cott's sex fantasies that Otto had shared over lunch: Cott dressed as an anime school girl, spanking parties, dominatrixes…

He didn't shut down his laptop until the cleaning staff arrived outside his office. He decided to walk home though it was well past midnight. Maybe the frosty air would clear his head.

When he reached Parliament Street, he thought of the vet clinic. Had Dr. Ali's staff put up a notice about Tiddles? Might as well check since he was here.

Business at Peepers strip club was brisk. Its brass doors stood open despite the chill, a crowd of patrons smoking outside. The loud throb of pop music assailed his ears as he passed under the pulsating lights of its marquee. Weaving his way around the smokers, something caught his eye.

He stopped in the middle of the sidewalk and stared.

I've been had!

***

Directly across the street from Peepers stood a Lebanese café. Thankfully it was still open. Amdur nabbed a seat by the front window where he had a full view of Peepers' brass doors. Shortly after he polished off his falafel, he spotted her leaving.

She strolled a short distance up Parliament and turned onto Winchester, the same street where he'd fled the lion two nights before.

He left the café and chased after her.

She seemed preoccupied. All to the good, since he was a complete novice at spying. He kept pace half a block behind her, dodging the recycling bins set out for next day's waste collection.

At the end of Winchester, she veered north onto Sumach Street. He raced to the corner only to find that she'd vanished. He swore in frustration.

The ground floor lights of the corner house flashed on — the same house where he'd stood watching the lion. Did she live *there*?

He remembered holding onto the black iron fence that encircled the house's front garden. But its back garden lay hidden by a high brick wall. Interesting...

He heard an outside door squeak open. And a voice, unmistakably hers, speaking in warm, affectionate tones.

"Did you miss me, Cyrano? Did you, baby?"

He had to see into that garden. He seized a nearby recycling bin and wheeled it over to the brick wall. In an ungainly scramble, he heaved himself onto the bin's lid. Leaning on his knees, he grasped the top of the rough brick wall and looked down into the garden.

And saw the lion!

The beast frolicked in the snow like an oversized dog. When she called his name, he bounded up to her and rubbed his huge mane against the navy legs of her police uniform.

"Good evening," Amdur called down from his perch. "Now I know where *you* live."

The lion turned. His yellow eyes gleamed, a ridge of the fur bristled down his back. He let out an unearthly roar that rattled nearby windows.

"Cyrano, no!" she shouted.

The lion crouched, ready to spring. Amdur lost his balance. In an explosion of noise, he flew off the recycling bin and crashed down on the icy sidewalk. He stared at the stars, winded, unable to move. Waiting for the dread dark shape of the carnivore to leap over the wall.

He heard her anxious voice call: "Cyrano! Cyrano!" Followed by the lion's roars and grunts as it loped back and forth on the other side of the wall.

Got to get out of here...got to. Before it jumps over and gets me.

His right knee hurt like a bastard. He rolled onto his side and dragged himself up.

Got to get home.

He limped down to the street corner. Now to get past the lion's house.

He heard the front door bang open.

"Wait, wait! Are you all right?" She charged down the verandah steps to intercept him.

He waved her off. "I'll be fine. Just keep that bloodthirsty animal of yours locked up. Now get out of my way. I've had a bloody awful day."

"Please don't call the police."

"Why not? You impersonated a police officer. And you're keeping a dangerous predator in a neighbourhood full of children."

"Cyrano's a sweetheart. He's completely tame. And I never said I was a cop."

"You led me on – admit it."

"All right, yes, I did. But I was desperate. I had to save Cyrano. The police would have shot him on sight."

Amdur couldn't argue with that. "He was behind the bushes the other night, wasn't he?"

"Yes, but he would never have hurt you. He's gentle and affectionate. Why don't you come in and see for yourself? I put him back in his cage. You'll be safe, I swear."

"To find out first hand if he likes human flesh? No, thank you!"

"At least tell me if Boots is all right."

"You mean the poor cat you threw at me? Obviously he's yours, too. Or was. Well, he's my cat now. And his name is Tiddles."

She started to cry. "I'm sorry. I'm so, so sorry. I didn't know what else to do. I had to get you out of the park before anyone else saw Cyrano. And-and now I've lost Boots…Tiddles…"

"At least he won't end up as an aperitif for Cyrano."

"NO! Cyrano would never hurt him. They're best friends. Look, Cyrano and I are going back to Las Vegas in a couple of days. I landed a six month gig. Can we please talk about this?"

"Fine". And so, against all his better instincts, Amdur gave in.

***

Sophie – for that was her name – settled him in the spacious kitchen at the back of the corner house. She placed an ice pack on his knee and a glass of Bourbon in his hand.

Cyrano crouched in a cage-like structure that resembled an oversized dog crate. He threw off a fusty, gamy odour that filled the room – indeed the entire house. The corner mansion, Amdur learned, belonged to Sophie's aunt who'd moved into a retirement home.

"I miss Boots," she said, wiping her eyes. "I found him in the park last June. He was starving. I nursed him back to health."

"You mean to say that you and Cyrano have been living in Riverdale for *six months*?"

She nodded. "We were between jobs."

"That cage looks flimsy." Amdur and Cyrano glowered at each other. "Small wonder he got out."

"It's my fault. Cyrano gets so bored cooped up in his cage. I let him have free run of the house sometimes. He's never caused trouble before. The other night I forgot to lock the front door. So he got out. Boots, too. Cyrano knows how to work door knobs. He's very intelligent."

As if on cue, the lion emitted a low vibrating growl.

"You hear that? He's purring." She refilled Amdur's glass. "I raised him from a cub. My folks, well, we're all circus people." She sighed. "I suppose you saw my photo outside Peepers."

"Yes, Sergeant Cupid, I did. Your police officer act is very convincing."

"I'm not ashamed. Pole dancing keeps me in shape. And it costs a lot to feed Cyrano." She frowned. "So are you going to turn me in?"

Amdur sighed. It was Christmas after all. "Fine, I keep Tiddles. You keep Cyrano. But first you're going to help me with something. To turn the worms in Ontario's biggest bait shop!"

***

"I'm an ADM in the Ontario government's largest ministry. I can't believe I let you talk me into this." Judy's hands danced along the rim of her van's steering wheel. Their wait at the Bay Street intersection outside Queen's Park was proving endless.

"Sorry about the short notice." Amdur said from the passenger seat. "You're the only one I could trust." His stomach burned. He'd worked through the night, fueled by endless espressos – and now this. "This was *not* part of the plan, believe me."

Behind them, Cyrano yawned, bathing them in sulfurous breath. At least a sturdy metal grille separated him from driver and passenger.

Sophie snickered from where she sat beside her lion. "Cyrano's just a big pussy cat, aren't you, big boy?"

Judy coughed. "I can't believe this. Driving a lion through morning rush hour traffic. In my cat rescue van. A lion!"

"I already told your buddy, Amdur, here. I can't leave Cyrano alone. He nearly got out again last night. Where I go, he goes. Or the deal's off."

"What deal?"

"The less you know about it, the better," Amdur put in.

"Ben, whatever you're planning, drop it. There are a thousand ways this will screw up. And you, Sophie, you should be thrown off the police force. We'll all end up in jail. This will kill Mother."

"No one is going to jail." Amdur wished he could feel more certain about that. "And Sophie's not a cop. She's a stripper."

"Oh, God." Judy leaned her forehead on the steering wheel. "I'm losing it."

"No, you are not losing it. Breathe deep. In, out." Amdur rested his hand on her back. "Come on now, in and out. You've faced down coyotes attacking lost cats. You can do this."

"Green light!" Sophie cried.

Horns blared behind them. Judy tromped on the accelerator. Amdur crashed back against his seat as they tore across the intersection.

Cyrano's claws scrabbled for purchase on the metal floor. He let out a bellow of fear. Sophie yelled and dragged on his chain.

The van swerved left, fish tailed down into darkness and slammed to a halt. Amdur hit the dash. Somehow, miraculously, Judy had steered them into the underground parking garage.

"Are you crazy!" Sophie shouted. "Cyrano get down! Cyrano!"

The lion let out an ear-shattering roar. Judy's screams matched his.

"Shut up! Shut up or this whole thing is off!" Sophie shouted.

"Everyone calm down!" Heart thumping, Amdur groped through the glove box and yanked out Judy's secret stash of scotch. "You, drink this." Judy seized the bottle, tore off the cap and sucked on it like oxygen. "And you, Sophie, control that bloody animal!"

Sophie glared at him. Cyrano moved restlessly, clinking his chain. They waited in strained silence until, after a long huff, the lion dropped back down.

"We're wasting precious time." Amdur checked his Blackberry. "All right, Otto has turned off the security cameras. Down to the freight bay."

"OK." Judy shoved the scotch bottle between her knees. She restarted the van and drove down to the next level.

They pulled into the deserted cargo bay. Ludmilla appeared on the loading platform.

Sophie gasped. "A cop!"

"It's all right. She's one of us." He acknowledged Ludmilla's thumbs-up. "Sophie and I are off now. Be ready to roll when I text you." Amdur gave Judy's arm a squeeze. "Remember, we're saving the health care of 14 million people."

"Fine, just leave me the scotch." Judy clutched the bottle to her chest.

Amdur jumped out of the van. He slid back the side door to release Sophie and Cyrano.

The lion sniffed the air, wrinkling his face at the smell of exhaust and gasoline. At Sophie's command he leaped onto the landing of the cargo bay. Amdur and Sophie followed him by way of the stairs.

Ludmilla gave Cyrano the once-over. "Nice lion. Beautiful animal. You feed him today, little girl?"

"He's perfectly tame!"

"Too bad. Maybe he change his mind when he sees Cott's fat ass."

She unlocked the freight elevator door with a grin. Amdur, Sophie and Cyrano climbed aboard. The door closed in front of them with a loud clang. The elevator lurched into motion, heading toward the top floor and the minister's office.

"Got your iPhone?" he asked Sophie. "Let's run through things one more time."

"Leave it! I know what to do." She frowned. "After today, we're done. Forever."

"Agreed."

"If this screws up, I won't be the only one going to jail. That's a promise."

"It'll be worth it." Amdur checked his phone. The message read: "Meeting full."

"What meeting?" Sophie read his screen without apology.

"It means we're safe for the moment. Everyone on the top floor is gone."

"Gone where?"

"To the farewell Christmas party for Vladimir Nickle, our old deputy minister. In my office, next floor down." The elevator bumped to a stop. "Here we are."

The doors rolled open. Faint sounds from Nickle's party trickled up the emergency stairwell to their left.

Amdur put the freight elevator on hold. He moved down to the end of the hallway and looked around the corner. The empty main corridor stretched down to the glass security barrier fronting the Minister's office. Outside it stood Cott's bodyguard.

"Damn!"

"What's going on?" Sophie pressed up behind him with a rattle of Cyrano's chain.

"Cott's bodyguard is still here."

"I'll take care of him. You hold Cyrano." She handed Amdur the leash. "Baby, lie down. I'll be back soon."

The lion grunted and sprawled on the floor. Sophie straightened her police uniform and strolled down to the Minister's office.

The bodyguard didn't speak until she reached the glass barrier. "Something wrong, officer?" Without the normal background office noise, his voice carried.

"Yes, I have an urgent message for Minister Cott from the Premier's office," Sophie said.

"OK, I'll give it to him."

"No can do. A Christmas card. From the Tory party. It's personal."

"Oh, right." The guard sounded weary. "I get it. *That* kind of Christmas card."

"We need some privacy, say 15 minutes. Can you fix that?"

"Yeah, I guess."

Amdur listened to the man's footsteps retreat. A heartbeat later he heard the swoosh of the main elevator doors.

Cyrano howled and leaped up, jerking the lead out of Amdur's grip. He loped down the corridor with Amdur in pursuit. Sophie was halfway through the security barrier.

She stopped, propping up the door with her foot. "You were supposed to hold him!"

"He got away from me."

"Fine, he can come visit the big bad boss." She picked up the lion's chain.

"NO!" Amdur said in a hoarse whisper. "Cott has a cat phobia. If he sees Cyrano, he'll have a heart attack."

"I thought that was the idea. Fine, take Cyrano in there." She pointed to the women's washroom directly opposite to where they were standing. "And don't upset him." She tossed him the lion's lead. "Cyrano, walkies!"

Cyrano whimpered as she disappeared into the Minister's office. Amdur hauled on his chain. By the time he'd dragged the lion into the washroom and shut the door, his arms throbbed with pain.

"Stay there!" Cyrano took shelter under the row of sinks, his tail lashing. Heart thumping, Amdur checked his phone. No messages. The two of them glared at each other.

Five minutes passed.

Sophie bragged she could handle any man. He hoped she was right. He creaked open the washroom door and peered out. Not a sound escaped the Minister's office.

Cyrano's bristling mane bumped against his leg. "Stay there. Don't come near me." The lion curled his flaccid blue upper lip and bared his teeth

Amdur's phone went off with a shrill cry. Judy's name appeared on the screen.

"Ben, what's happening?" Her words sounded slurred. "I'm going crazy down here. The media people, they're already…"

Cyrano let out a low growl. It did not sound like purring.

"Shut up, you! No, not you, Judy."

His phone pinged. A message. He cut Judy off.

One word: "Help."

"Sophie!"

I can think of a thousand ways this could go wrong…

He sent an urgent text to Otto for the code to the security door.

Five more minutes passed. No reply.

Another message: "Help!"

Desperate now, he thought of the fire alarm.

"Cyrano, get up! Help Sophie. Come on, get up!" He tugged on the lion's chain.

He may as well have been reading Cyrano the ministry's annual report. The lion merely yawned and rested his massive head on his front paws.

"You miserable waste of space! Well, bloody stay there!" He dropped the chain and burst out of the washroom. Where the hell was the fire alarm?

"Help!" A scream from the Minister's office.

"Sophie!" He ran over to the barrier. Banged on the glass. Cyrano, trapped in the washroom, let out an echoing roar.

Two figures burst through the Minister's door. A police officer, her uniform torn open, revealing sexy red underwear. And a bulky man in a Japanese schoolgirl uniform brandishing a riding crop. Cott's pale hairy buttocks and drooping appendage were a sight that seared into one's memory.

"Open it! Open up!" Sophie crashed her fists against the glass door.

Amdur, powerless to help, shouted, "I see you, Cott. There's a witness."

Cott seized Sophie by the throat. "Gimme that phone, you bitch!"

Sophie tried to knee him in the crotch and missed.

Several things happened at once. The main elevator doors flew open and released a staggering Judy. Sophie thumped Cott in the eye. And Cyrano flew out of the washroom with a terrifying roar.

He leaped onto the security barrier. His forepaws hung over the top edge. His powerful hind legs scrabbled on the glass pane.

Otto, for God's sake!

Numbers appeared on Amdur's phone screen. He punched the code into the keypad. Tore open the security door.

Sophie burst free. Cott rushed after her, waving the riding crop. Amdur stuck out his foot.

Cott tripped and fell. "Gimme that phone." He scrabbled after Sophie.

Amdur kicked the security door shut, cutting off Cott's escape.

A slithering sound. Cyrano glided down from the glass barrier. He bounded toward them.

Cott let out an unearthly shriek of pure terror.

"No, Cyrano! No!" Sophie grabbed for his chain.

Cyrano's paw lashed through the air. Cott tumbled to the floor. The lion stood over him, drooling...

Sophie threw herself at Cyrano. Buried her face in his mane. Stroked his flanks.

"The media. They're here. They're on their way up." Judy choked out. "That's what I tried to tell you."

The lion's pink tongue spilled over his vile-looking fangs. He let out a woof, reluctant to abandon Cott's fat ass.

Sophie murmured to him. After what seemed like an eternity, Cyrano stepped away from Cott's trembling form.

"Get out of here! Run, Judy!" Amdur pushed her in the direction of the freight elevator. "Sophie, get that animal moving."

"Cyrano, gallop!"

Sophie dashed down the corridor. The lion streaked after her in a four-footed animal run.

The main elevators pinged. The doors opened. A full media crew poured out for the Minister's press conference, lights and video cameras at the ready.

Cott staggered up, his garish make-up hideous under his curly blond wig. He saw the reporters and screamed.

"Minister?"

Amdur beat a hasty retreat back down the corridor. A clamor of voices rose behind him. No time to stop. Back at the freight elevator, he turned the key and got it moving.

"Are you all right?"

Sophie nodded. She finished buttoning up her tunic and handed him her phone. "I want that back. And this never happened."

"Fair enough. Give me the keys to the van, Judy. You're in no condition to drive." She handed them over.

The elevator stopped. Ludmilla opened the door and signaled they were still in the clear.

He passed Judy's keys to Sophie. "Leave the van outside my place. You know where I live."

"Where are you going?"

"To Nickle's farewell Christmas party." He closed the elevator doors.

Back upstairs, he and Judy were engulfed by a crowd of partying civil serpents. They spilled out of Amdur's office, occupying every cubicle on the floor. Even Vladimir Nickle had abandoned his crusty sense of decorum. Surrounded by well-wishers, he gulped wine from a plastic glass, his Santa hat askew.

"I'm drunk," Judy whispered.

"No worries. So is everyone else."

Amdur located Otto by the buffet table . Potluck at the Ministry never failed to provide a feast: Otto's paper plate was folded in half under the weight of food.

"I especially recommend the lasagna, doctor."

"Here." Amdur slipped him Sophie's phone.

"Be back, one minute." Otto set down his plate and disappeared.

Amdur turned his attention to the wine table for a much-needed drink. He filled plates with food for him and Judy. A moment later, someone let out a shout by the window.

"Look! Some weirdo's running down Bay Street. There's a TV crew after him."

People crowded to that side of the room.

"Holy shit! It's Cott!" A man stood staring at his phone.

"He's on the government website, too!" A woman pointed to the computer beside her.

Phones and computer screens flashed on, food and wine temporarily forgotten. In the ensuing shock and awe, Otto returned and passed Sophie's phone back to Amdur.

"How did you do that?"

"Oh, a global internet tour via Mauritius. Untraceable. Better you should not ask, doctor." Otto helped himself to Christmas cake.

***

On Christmas night, Amdur settled back in his study, a glass of cognac in his hand and Tiddles on his lap, to watch his favorite holiday movie, *It's a Wonderful Life*. It certainly is, he thought. This is the best Christmas I've had in years.

The news story of Cott's resignation still had legs two weeks later. The video showcasing his misadventures had millions of hits on websites around the world. American comedy shows trumpeted his antics with actors dressed up as moose and beavers. For once Canadians weren't boring.

Amdur gave Tiddles a pat, happily digesting the Christmas dinner he'd enjoyed earlier with Judy and her mother. On the mantle over the fireplace stood two postcards, one showing a glittering burlesque show in Las Vegas, the other a beach in Mauritius.

Snowflakes drifted slowly past the windows of his flat. And if he stared long and hard enough into Riverdale Park, he imagined they formed the dancing figure of a lion.

Follow Madeleine's blog on her website at
www.mhcallway.com
and on Facebook and Twitter (@mcallway).

ABOUT THE AUTHOR

Margaret Cannon, crime fiction reviewer for the *Globe and Mail* called M. H. Callway "a writer to watch".

Many of Madeleine's stories and novellas have won or been short-listed for awards, including the Arthur Ellis, Derringer and Bony Pete Awards. Most recently, her novella, *Glow Grass*, was a finalist for the 2016 Arthur Ellis Best Novella Award.

Madeleine's debut novel, *Windigo Fire*, was published in September 2014 by Seraphim Editions. It was a finalist for the 2015 Arthur Ellis Award for Best First Novel and a *Huffington Post* Book for Book Clubs Selection. Prior to publication, under different titles, it was a runner-up for the Unhanged Arthur and the Debut Dagger Awards.

In 2013, Madeleine founded the Mesdames of Mayhem, a collective of 15 established Canadian women crime writers, publishers and editors.

www.ingramcontent.com/pod-product-compliance
Lightning Source LLC
Chambersburg PA
CBHW032115170626
46808CB00006B/1956